IN THE TIME OF LILACS

and

OTHER SHORT STORIES

Volume II

IN THE TIME OF LILACS

and

OTHER SHORT STORIES

Volume II

Christmas Carol Kauffman
Compiled by Marcia Kauffman Clark

DIGITAL
LEGEND

New York

Send inquiries to:

Digital Legend Press and Publishing
4700 Clover Street
Honeoye Falls, NY 14472

See the complete Digital Legend library, visit www.digitalegend.com

For info write to: info@digitalegend.com
or call toll free: 877-222-1960

ISBN: 978-1-934537-83-1

Printed in the United States of America
First Printing: October 2011 (V1)

Book interior format and cover design by Alisha Bishop

TABLE OF CONTENTS

CHRISTMAS CAROL KAUFFMAN
1901–1969

Christmas Carol Kauffman was born on December 25, 1901, in Elkhart, Indiana, the second daughter of Abraham Rohrer and Selena Bell Wade Miller. Carol, as she was known, graduated from Elkhart High School and attended both Hesston and Goshen Colleges. She began writing short stories at Hesston College and continued writing one short story per month for the *Youths Christian Companion*. In total, she wrote more than one hundred short stories.

In 1929 she married Nelson Edward Kauffman. They served together at the Hannibal Mission Church in Missouri for twenty-two years, where Nelson was the pastor. They are parents of four children.

While in Hannibal, Carol began writing book-length inspirational true stories that were published by Herald Press. *Lucy Winchester,* her first book, was published in 1945. Throughout the next two decades she authored six additional books: *Light from Heaven* (1948), Dannie of Cedar Cliffs (1950), Not Regina (1954), Hidden Rainbow (1957), For One Moment (1960), and Search *to Belong* (1963). After her death, two more books were published in 1971: *Little Pete and Other Stories* a collection of thirteen of her short stories, originally written in 1928 and *One Boy's Battle,* written in 1948 and originally titled *Unspoken Love*. All nine of her books continue to be published today.

Christmas Carol Kauffman died on January 30, 1969.

FOREWORD

C hristmas Carol Kauffman, as a writer, was able to transform a difficult, unfortunate, unfair situation into a glorious testimony of God's love, provision, and redemption. Her writings captivated her readers and touched their lives in a way to inspire them to move on with a deeper relationship with God. What a gift that lives on forever!

When I was a child, about nine years old, I remember eagerly awaiting the arrival of the Youths Christian Companion each month to read Carol's stories. I especially remember reading "Lucy Winchester," always ready for the next chapter. I never dreamed that I would one day, many years later, be working in her home and typing part of a book for her. I arrived as Nelson, her husband's, secretary at the time when she was putting the finishing touches on "Not Regina" and starting "Hidden Rainbow." As one friend put it to me, "It must be great living in a town with writers past (Mark Twain) and present, Carol." It was.

Carol had a vivid imagination that carried her into countless situations that she was able to weave into a story with a deep-reaching spiritual application—simply and beautifully. I can understand her need to scrawl as she endeavored to capture every thought as it rushed by her. And why she needed to seclude herself as much as possible while writing. Carol always had time for her children when they needed her. I'm sure there were times when she would have been happy just to be alone with her family and caring for them. Sometimes we didn't see very much of her for a while. So it was our great pleasure to have her accompany us to a concert or event occasionally. Carol's need to write was a driving force in her life, a God-given gift. She truly was a literary fore-runner in the Mennonite Church.

The last time my husband and I visited Carol was in Elkhart, Ind. on November 22, 1962, when we learned that President John F. Kennedy had been assassinated. She was home alone at the time. It was very difficult to wrap our minds such a devastating situation. She was so compassionate.

How wonderful that, after leaving the responsibilities of the Hannibal Mission, she would be able to teach an intermediate class of students in Sunday School, directly influencing their lives, pouring her life into theirs. As a retired minister's wife, attending and working in another church, I can see her just beaming. Imagine the future of the children who had the good fortune to be her students! Not only do her writings live on, but her life, also.

I will always remember Carol's deep faith and her willingness to bring us all together for Nelson's radio broadcast every Sunday morning, for prayer when someone had a need, her ability to join in fun, especially when we could get her husband, Nelson, to put on an act as a mimic. This rarely happened, though, and we found it an insight into his personality. There must have been some hilarious moments in their life together.

When I considered the foreword finished, I reached over to my bookshelf and picked up one of Carol's books. I started to read and I just could not put it down. It was like reading a new book. Her writings are timeless and as interesting as any book written today. They promote wonderful Christian principals and values. There certainly was am enabling grace on her work.

What a pleasure it is to have our little Marcia grown up and walking in her Mother's footsteps as a writer. Thank you, Marcia, for sharing insight into your Mother's life of which we probably would never have been aware.

Ruth King Wall
Calgary, Alberta

PREFACE

*C*arol was born at 6am Christmas morning 108 years ago. The stories in Volume II were written when she was between the ages of 28 to 31, or 80 to 83 years ago, and were published only once.

My husband Stephen and I had the privilege of spending several days including Christmas Day with two of our children and their families in Michigan. As soon as the Goshen College Historical Library was reopened after the holiday break, we were able to spend four days leafing through fifteen large bound volumes, each including two years of weekly published *Youth's Christian Companions* from 1928 through 1956. The large heavy books were so tightly bound that when photocopied the inside margin left a long black, fuzzy, unreadable line from the middle margin of each page. Because of this we also took digital pictures of each page, to hopefully capture unreadable words. Some of the photographs were very difficult to read, requiring a magnifying glass to read the computer prints out. Some of the volumes were so tightly bound in the center that even the camera did not capture needed words. It was very time consuming to type these precious gems for you, but very rewarding. Therefore a few of the words chosen by me to make up a sentence may or may not be exactly what Carol wrote, but most are her carefully chosen words that grab your heart strings and keep them tightly bound till the very last word. Carol said that whenever she started a new story, she needed to know what the last sentence was going to be before she started writing the first. This is very evident because each story becomes a full circle for the reader. It is with deepest gratitude that I have the privilege of bringing you this second volume.

Two chapters in this book are not stories but articles which likewise express her true nature. In number 40, "Motives for Education," she shared her practiced inner beliefs. Carol's true self is very evident through her written statement: "Motives, however, may vary, but to the Christian they must be always good and pure and tend to develop not only the physical and mental, but also the spiritual life for the influence of good."

Carol truly preached what she practiced. During her entire life, within her God given gift of writing, both her short stories and full length novels, left readers without any doubt of what she truly believed and practiced. In the last part of the same article she wrote: "We must give our lives, our energy, our enthusiasm to the highest, of which we are capable. There is only one real failure in life possible, and that is not to be true to the best we know. It is of great value to have a motive, and to the Christian that motive is good and pure. Our motive for an education then should be just the same as the motive for every other act in life, that all our abilities be fully consecrated and increased for the service of the Master."

In the midst of Carol's responsibilities as Nelson's devoted wife, she found the needed time to create from her phenomenal mind each of these "one of a kind" stories you are about to read. Her eight full length novels had the same underlying theme; expressing what she desired the readers to understand and accept. They all were written with every individual reader in mind, to accept and become determined to create an even more devoted Christ centered life, because of what each story taught.

For some unknown reason, Mother had the underling fear that people would make fun of her and that her stories might not be good enough to be accepted and published. It was her personal fear, but I think it kept her humble, prayerful and teachable; an attribute very few authors acquire, who become as well known as Christmas Carol was many years ago and still is today in 2010.

I express appreciation and gratitude for both my publisher Boyd J. Tuttle, for his continuing interest in Mother's "one time" published stories, and to Alisha Tuttle Bishop, his daughter who designed the layout and cover of this book. Joe Springer offered

2

and gave me very kind assistance at the Goshen College Historical Library. Without Joe's interest and help you would not be holding this priceless book in your hand. Many thanks again, Joe. I also wish to again thank Joshua Byler, from the Mennonite Publishing Network for granting me permission to republish these touching stores for a new generation of readers. I have very fond memories of having Ruth King live in our home. She was also like a precious big sister to me as was Esther Stoltzfus, who wrote the Forward for Volume I. Both were loving "workers" in our mission home in Hannibal, Missouri. Ruth, how grateful I am for your wonderful forward for this second volume. We three have priceless memories to cherish together. I wish we could relive some of those happy days along with Mother near at hand, busy with her lead pencils at the ironing board adjusted for her 4' 11" height, as she created a building plot that keeps us desiring more and more of her stories to read again and again.

Each story engages you from the very first sentence and holds your undivided attention till the very last word. I also express gratitude for C. F. Yake, the editor of *The Youth's Christian Companion* who recognized in Carol a treasured writing talent in 1928. Each and every ability of Carol's was used as she shared her gift then and now with us today. She increased and consecrated her personal gift for the service of our Lord and Master, practicing what she wrote about when a student at Hesston College. She desired that we also individually consecrate our best for the Lord.

I again share my sincere gratitude for having the privilege of calling Carol, Mother. Thank you Mother for being true to the best you knew; true to your beliefs with a motive to be good and pure and for your desire to develop your mental and spiritual life for the influence for good upon many thousands, including me.

Marcia Kauffman Clark

THE TRUTH SHALL MAKE YOU FREE

By Carol Hostetler, age 26 Hesston College, Hesston Kansas
Originally published August 12, 1928,
in the Youth's Christian Companion

Alfred had just entered his room and was ripping off his necktie with a jerk, at the same time kicking his one shoe into the farther corner of the room. Every move he made, every sound he uttered, and most of all his countenance showed he was miserably burdened and oppressed. Just as he was about to turn out the light, his head turned with a jerk, and he sprang to the window. On the street below someone was passing with light, quick steps, and through the night air came the clear sound of his voice whistling, "There is within my soul a melody."

"Well, that sounds like Jim."

At the same time Alfred leaned out of the upstairs window and whistled his old familiar call. Instantly the figure on the walk stopped and gave his answer.

"Hi, there Jim. When did you get home?

"About four-thirty this afternoon. Come on down. I've got lots to tell you."

In a moment the boys were gripping each other's hands in a hearty shake.

"I say Jim, you're looking fine and robust. That dormitory life must have done you good. Or did you just lie around and take life easy? Confess now."

"Lie around nothing. I never worked so hard in all my life, and to tell you the truth I rather enjoyed it."

"That sounds quite different from the letter you wrote me the first week you were there."

"Ha, 'quite different", is right. I was furious when I left home. You know Dad sent me to Hesston when I wanted to stay here and go to high school with you and Tom. I never did fancy the idea of a Church school. Well, they put me in a room with a college freshman, and that fellow won my confidence the first week. Not the first night, however. When the ten-minute bell rang, he opened his Bible and started to read out loud. I had to listen. But it made me crosser than ever when he asked me to lead in prayer. Me, lead in prayer! Can you imagine that, Alfred? My tongue felt tied and my mind was in a whirl and all I could say was, "Dear Lord—Dear Lord—" and cough and stutter "Amen." And say, Alfred, he never let on, but the next time he called me, I had something to say. He took me along to prayer circle, literary, and devotional, and before I knew it, I actually became interested in those meetings. Really, Alfred, I never knew that the Bible was for fellows to read. The teachers make it real to a person. Sister was in the same class with me and we've got the same experience to tell. Wait till you see her.

"One Sunday afternoon we took a long walk down to the grove and she said to me, "Jimmy, I'm going to stand up to-night if they give an invitation. I can't wait another day. I want to be free—free."

My heart took a leap, for that was what I was about to say. That night Brother D. H. Bender, our president, gave an invitation and Sister and I stood up and I said, "Alfred, something new came into my life or something old went out. But I've been free ever since."

"Free from what?" asked Alfred. His face even in the moonlight was drawn and sad.

"Free from sin, free from care and from a guilty conscience."

"Well, you've got something I don't have, I guess, because life is nothing but drudgery for me. Work and not enough pay in an envelope, and more work.

"You're living in a cage, Alfred, you're all penned up with your gloomy thoughts and sins. That's just the way I felt when I went to Hesston but now I'm free. Their school motto is, "The Truth Shall Make You Free." That was Greek to me, until I began reading the Bible, but now it's easy to understand. God is truth, and if you believe and accept it, you are free. You're going along back to Hesston with me next year, Alfred?

"Don't be funny, Jim."

"You are. I'm going to speak to Father in the morning. Two and a half months and we'll be traveling west together.

Alfred shifted from one foot to another and smiled faintly. He ran his hand through his hair and said, "Speak to Father if you like."

** *Both Carol and Nelson, ten months before they were married on June 10, 1929 were asked to write articles about Hesston College, that were printed on the same publication dated. Nelson's was an article. Carol's, not to my surprise, was written in story form.*

—Marcia Kauffman Clark.

7

TWO MORE POINTS

By Carol Hostetler age 27, 1929
Hesston College Hesston, Kansas
Originally published May 19, and 26 1929
in the Youth's Christian Companion

The man under the cherry tree painting the canoe looked up in surprise when a chubby, freckle-faced boy without a cap entered from the farther end of the garden and seated himself on the cistern near by. He was munching at an apple which he held in one hand. In the other he held a bunch of small pamphlets. He laid them down on the cistern beside him, pulled out a slightly soiled handkerchief and wiped the perspiration from his forehead.

"Hello stranger." With his brush in his hand, the man stepped back a few feet and scrutinized his work with an air of critical satisfaction. The front of his shirt was generously decorated with red paint. This he also eyed with half satisfaction. He turned to the boy on the cistern.

"How's that, Bud, for a nice-looking job?"

"Good enough," was the ready response.

"Your boat?"

"Yep I just finished it last night."

The boy's eyes opened wide. He came over, stooped down and looked into the canoe as it rested upside down on the two sawhorses. He examined the seats, the lining, the joints. He asked questions and more questions. He touched the paint to see if—well, why do boys touch wet paint anyway? Yes, it was still subject to impression.

"Make it yourself?"

The man laid his brush on the end of the sawhorse, tossed his head in the air, and laughed good-naturedly. "Greatest sport I ever knew. The only thing I'll like better is to paddle her for the first time."

"How soon do you suppose it will be dry enough to use?"

"By tonight." The man pulled his watch from his pocket and replaced it immediately.

"Four-fifteen already. Want to put on a coat of Valspar in the morning soon as I get home."

"Where from?"

"Work, boy."

"Where you work?"

"Shell Station."

"Guess that's what I'll do. Like it?"

"Like this better, Bud. The man resumed his work with new enthusiasm.

"Ever had a ride in one?"

"Once." The boy's eyes fairly danced.

"Like it?"

"Bet your life. My uncle in Michigan can paddle as straight and smooth as a swallow flies."

"What's your name, brother?" The man rather liked this freckle-faced stranger.

"Merle. What's yours?"

"Hardly know, Merle. Got so many names. Used to call me Sonny when I was near your size, then it was Dannie for a while till' made 'em leave off the "nie'. Was Zip in High School, Slim, and Kinky." Here the man laughed again and shook his head so that some of the loose kinky locks fell over his damp forehead. "Call me any one of them you like except Kinky. Guess Dan's the name I hear mostly. Just moved into the neighborhood, Merle?"

The boy shook his head. "Nope." Live over by the viaduct in that yellow house. Know where I mean?"

"Why—I go down that way to work. The place where all those tulips are in blossom, along the front walk and around the house?"

"That's it." The boy stepped a little closer and watched Dan spread the crimson paint.

"Sure nice—them flowers. Took mother past there last night and she went into raptures over them. Said we're goina have some too next year."

There was a little pile of pamphlets on the cistern over in the yard. Merle dashed here and there in a desperate effort to collect them. One blew against the freshly painted canoe and stuck there. Dan Fink snatched it off, crumpled it and threw it to the ground in anger. He would rather have lost a day's wages than to have the pride of his two week's afternoon labor marred or scratched. It dare not be! He simply could not tolerate it! Turning on Merle, he said in a rather harsh voice.

"Gather up those papers and keep them in your pocket or throw them in the fire. I think there ought to be a city ordinance against the peddling of advertisements. Nobody ever reads them anyway."

"These aren't advertisements, they're—"

"Well, whatever they are they're a nuisance and do more harm than good."

He stroked his wet brush over the place where the paper had fastened itself. A deep color of wrath rose to his face. Could it be that this jolly good-natured man could get angry over a little thing like that? Merle looked at him in dumb amazement. He had all the papers gathered up now and started off toward the garden path, then turned and came over to Dan.

"Sorry it happened sir. Hope it won't leave a mark.

Of course it didn't leave a mark and Dan Fink knew it, but the incident irritated him nevertheless.

"What are they anyway?" He snapped.

"These?" Merle looked at the bunch of slightly crumpled papers in his left hand.

"Why, they're tracts, Kink—I mean Dan."

"That's better, boy. Tracts?"

"Yes sir. Eldon Berger, teacher of our class, had us meet in the lecture room Sunday after Church an' gave each of us fellows fifty of these to give out by Friday night. We're going to have a wiener roast that night an' give a report. I gave out twenty-two this week so far." He handed one of the papers to Dan.

"Here, this makes the twenty-third. We're supposed to invite folks to Church an', if they promise to come, that gives us one point. If they become a regular member of our Sunday School it gives us two points, and if they confess—a—become a Christian—in a year—they get a star. That's why it takes all week to pass out fifty. Can't always think o' nothin' to say to folks." Merle shifted from one foot to the other and bit his lip nervously.

Dan Fink made no effort to take the tract the boy held out to him.

"Well, you've wasted pretty near half an hour on me, then young man. Run into the house and make your speech to my mother. I'm not the least bit interested. This job here is all I can manage. See? I'm going to launch her out Saturday or I'll—"

The man did not finish his sentence. With the can of paint in his one hand, and the brush in the other he stepped back to once more view his work. He put his foot on an empty spool hidden in the grass. His ankle turned, his arm jerked and the can of paint fell to the ground, leaving a big blotch of red where it fell. His face grew almost white with anger.

***

"Say, I'll run up town and get another can for you, Dan. Shall I?" Then you can get it done tonight."

"Here." Dan reached in his pocket and drew out a dollar bill. Go to Jenken's Hardware basement. Ask for Mr. Vardon. Tell him to give you a can of paint like Dan Fink got yesterday. He knows. Here, give me those pesky papers till you come back. I'll go on with what's left."

Dan laid the tracts on the cistern, put a brick on top of them, went into the house for a drink and returned.

"The little rascal," he said to himself. Just for fun I'll read one of these things."

He lifted the corner of the brick, pulled out one of the papers and read. A cynical smile crossed his flushed face. "A week too late. A lady in Scotland was so troubled one night about her soul that she could not rest, and got up and wrote in her diary, 'One year from now I will attend to the matter of the salvation of my soul.' She went to bed but could not sleep. So she rose again and wrote. 'One month from now I will attend to the salvation of my soul.' Then she slept. The next day she went into scenes of gaiety. The following day she was sick; and by the middle of the week she was dead. Delirium left her mind just long enough to say, "I am a week too late! I am lost!"

Dan Fink cleared his throat. He looked around half sheepishly to see if anyone was watching him. Now, no one was in sight, not even the dog. He turned the paper over and read.

"Which will you lose? One night at a revival meeting a 'young man was urged to repent.' He said, 'I will tomorrow night'.

The next evening, his mother found him getting ready to go skating, and begged him not to go, but go along to the revival instead. 'I will go if I die.' He answered. He went upstairs for his skates. His chum arrived and whistled for him.

He did not come down. His mother went to the stair door and called. He did not answer. She went up to his room, and found his lifeless body on the floor. He lost the startling chance to change his life and repent. Which are you going to loose? Christ in His glory or the pleasures of earth which will crumble at the appearance of Christ like the dust on a rainy day?

Dan Fink returned the tract to the place where he got it, picked up his brush and went to work. He did not notice Merle coming down the street on a trot.

"Here you are, Dan." Merle laid the can of paint on the end of the sawhorse and sank to the cistern with a puff. "Pretty hot today."

"Yes—yes, thanks Merle. Good sport, thanks. Now take your papers and run along. Think I can finish now before sundown."

Merle handed over the forty cents of change.

"Keep it kid—Keep it. Mighty glad to help get the paint. No—never mind. Keep it. Run along or you won't get that bunch passed out by Friday night."

"And you won't take one sir?" He held out one wistfully.

"Don't care for it, Bud. Can't be bothered."

"Well, so long—Dan. Thanks for the tip."

Merle walked off jingling the change in his pants pocket. He stopped at the grocery store at the end of the block and bought an ice cream cone. He managed to get rid of one of the tracts there.

By sundown Dan Fink had finished painting the canoe, and was getting ready for work. This was his week to work nights at the filling station. The next evening he put on the coat of Valspar.

Saturday morning came in golden spender. Dan never felt better in his life. Everyone he met seemed in good humor, even old Duke Forbes. The tulips in front of the big yellow house by the viaduct seemed to bloom especially for him.

Every customer he waited on that morning heard that Dan has a new canoe and was going to launch her for the first time that very afternoon.

The dinner just suited Dan: French fried potatoes, veal chops, gravy, cabbage salad. The custard pie was excellent and he told his mother so.

Off in the distance a low rumbling was heard. The sun seemed to be growing a little less bright, but Dan did not notice. The sky grew suddenly dark; the curtains at the open window fluttered strangely and the leaves of the cherry trees outside turned up and showed their light sides; the cat at the front door mewed pitifully. All this Dan noticed! He walked out on the porch and looked north. A black cloud, a monstrous black cloud was making its way toward him in cruel mockery. He could not stop it. He would have, if he could have.

Great drops splashed on the sidewalk, children ran into their houses, cars passing raised up their windows, and Dan's mother turned on the electric lights. A sharp stinging crash was heard. It seemed to be in the near distance. The lights went out for a few minutes, then flickered on again. The rain fell fast now. Not a child was in sight. Now it poured in great transparent sheets. Only a few cars passed and those drove by very slowly. Dan mumbled something under his breath, walked into the house and shut the door with a bang. The telephone rang. Dan answered.

***

"Did you Dan?"
"Yes," The voice was husky and strangely anxious.
"Did you hear the crash a bit ago?"
"Yes."

"Lightning struck that pole here beside the station and knocked Art over. He's unconscious. I called for help but—Dan, you call up his mother and tell her—I—can't."

"Oh Rex!"

"Come on Dan, do it right away."

The receiver at the other end of the line clicked. Dan stood in amazement. Mrs. Fink ran into the room.

"What Dan?" Tell me." She could not understand the strange troubled look on his face. She came up and caught him by his arm. "Tell me Dan,"

Lightning struck the pole by the station. Art is unconscious. Rex wants me to call up Art's mother. I can't. You do it.

He stepped to the closet and pulled on his raincoat.

"Where are you going, Dan?"

"Down to the station."

"In this storm?" No Dan."

"Why certainly, mother." And he ran down over the steps.

Art was conscious when Dan got there, but he looked white—terribly white and strange. The doctor had been there and left his orders. Art tried to smile at Dan when he came in, but it was more of a grimace than a smile.

"Take your boat out?"

"Like your playing golf."

"Say Dan," Art's hands shook and he could scarcely speak. "S'pose you'll think I'm crazy, but first thing I thought of when I came to was what I said to a kid this morning.

"What was that, Art?"

"Why a kid tried to give me a tract and I swore at him—and told him the only time they'd get me into a Church would be when they carry me in my casket."

The same worried expression crossed the face of Dan Fink.

"Must have been the same kid that talked to me on Thursday afternoon. Chubby—freckles?"

"Yeh—kinda cute kid?"

"Was at that. I—I told him I'd go out in my canoe today or—well I didn't just say but I meant what you did."

"Call a taxi, Dan. I'm sick. Weak as pebble broth. Doc said I should go to bed; and I won't have to be coaxed much."

Dan called the taxi. He had to almost carry Art to the cab. They sat in dumb silence for several blocks.

"What you thinkin' about. Dan?"

"Did you read the kids tract?"

"No. Why, what was it?"

"Can't remember right, but something about a man who said he'd go skating if he died and he did."

"Did what?" Art clenched his fists.

"Didn't go alive. Wish I had taken one. Know where the kid lives—freckle face chap."

The driver put on the brakes and stopped in front of Art's home. Two half-hysterical women ran out onto the porch. Dan leaned out of the car in the rain and called. "He's all right, Mrs. Brown. Just frightened."

"Oh," was the thankful response.

That evening shortly after dark when the storm was over, and the whole earth sparkled, laughed, and sang in all her beauty, a car stopped in front of the big yellow house by the viaduct, and a tall, well-dressed man swung up the walk between the tulips, and rapped at the screen door. A little woman in a pink gingham house dress answered the knock.

"Good evening, madam. Pardon me, but do you have a son by the name of Merle?"

"I do yes," was the pleasant reply.

"Is he here?"

"He is in his room, yes. Won't you step in?" I'll call him." She opened the stair door and called.

"Merle, O Merle! There's a gentleman here to see you."

"Hello, Merle." Dan Fink stepped forward and held out his big hand. For an instant Merle's face wore a puzzled expression. Then suddenly a radiant smile crossed his freckled face.

"Why, it's Dan Fink. I didn't hardly know you in those clothes."

"S'pose I do look a little different than I did in the back yard the other day."

"Won't you take a chair, Mr. Fink?" Merle's mother spoke.

"No thank you. Must be going at once. Have a sick friend I want to call on yet this evening. Quite a storm we had today."

"Indeed it was."

"I just came in to tell you, Merle, that you can count on two more points. I'll be there tomorrow morning and bring my friend if he's able and if not tomorrow, we'll be there next Sunday. Do you have one of those—" Dan Fink cleared his throat, walked to the door and said good night.

"Say Dan", called Merle, "Did you take your canoe out yet?"

"That's yet to come, Merle. And you're going with me."

THE ALTAR OF LOVE

By Carol Hostetler Kauffman, age 28,
Hesston College Hesston, Kansas
Originally published March 30, 1930
in the Youth's Christian Companion

"Julia," Someone touched the girl lightly on the shoulder. She turned abruptly.

"How did you come, Julia?"

"I walked. Father had to work again tonight and Ed—well he—"

"Well, you can't start out in this storm. I thought I didn't see any of your folks here to-night. Just wait a minute, we'll take you home."

"Oh, Treva, no! That's too—"

"No it isn't Julia. I couldn't think of seeing you start out without an umbrella."

"I thought maybe I could ride along with Wayman's, but I see they're gone already."

"Your mother will be anxious about you—Come on; here's our car."

Even on the most beautiful nights the mid-week Bible Class was poorly attended by the young folks of the Blue Valley Congregation. Was it the fault of the leader? Was it the fault of the young people? Didn't the parents of the forty-some young people between the ages of sixteen and twenty-five who were members of the church even try to see to it that they went? Didn't the young folks have any interest at all in any midweek meetings? They had plenty of interest in midweek, and any-part-of- the-week, parties. Something was wrong, but what was it? Some of the most serious-minded members had asked each other these questions only to receive for an answer a shake of the head, or "I'm sure I don't know," or "It does seem too bad. Brother Whitely drives twelve miles to teach this class and no more takes advantage of it." Some said it was the evening, so they changed that and still only a handful of young folks came. Some said the parents didn't show enough interest, and some said it was the spirit of the times. All young people were drifting, and so what could we expect?"

Every Thursday evening almost without exception the entire Brown family came in, father, mother, and six children, including the newest one who had to be carried. Treva looked after the next one, a curly-headed little fellow with mischief sticking out of both eyes. And Julia came whenever it was at all possible. Of course, there were times when she hated to leave her mother alone, and her father had to work over time so often. Ed just naturally—well he was always indisposed, or had another engagement, preferably the latter.

"This is surely kind of you folks to take me home to-night." Spoke Julia as she squeezed herself in the already crowded back seat.

"Always room for one more," laughed Mr. Brown good-naturedly. "Some rain, isn't it?"

"I never dreamed of such a thing when I left home."

"Your father working again?"

"Oh, yes, I do wish father could get a job where he wouldn't be tied down so. He would like to have come to-night?"

"How's your mother today, Julia?" Mrs. Brown had one of those kind, patient, never excited voices, which not enough mothers possessed. "Just sit still, Dale, we'll soon be home. Yes, I know, but I'm talking to Julia just now."

"Why, Mother felt better today. It was so spring-like to-day, you know; she felt so happy helping to plan the garden. The winter has been so long for her; you know she never got used to being shut in so long."

"I think Bro. Whitley has been giving us some wonderful lessons, don't you?"

"I surely do. If only more people who could, would come!"

"Well, what do you think is the reason?" asked Mrs. Brown.

"I'm sure I—" *Bang!* A side-sway on the pavement brought a bump and a stop.

"Well, can you beat that on a day like this."

"But Father," spoke Treva; "Look we're right in front of the house. You can't fix that tire in this pour-down. We'll just all wait. And Julia, you can stay here all night.

"Oh, Treva, I—"

"Sure, sure! Why not?" I'll call up your mother right away. I've been wanting to have you here over night for ever and ever, haven't I, Mother?"

"Yes, stay Julia; we'll see that you get to work in time. Just put the car in the garage, Will, and fix the tire in the morning."

A dry house, comfortable chairs, and shaded lights, the sound of a good spring rain, work all aside, the family gathered around in a circle, the baby breathing in sound sleep on her Mother's breast, and Dale on Father's lap. What a picture! Julia looked, with wondering eyes, at the order and decency in which every little tot behaved. But then, she was there. Perhaps they were taught to have manners becoming to company. Then Mr. Brown took from the table a well- worn, and much thumbed through Bible and began to read, not fluently, nor with any oratorical ability, but slowly, now and then repeating a word or two at first that seemed difficult to pronounce. But, what reverence! And with what reverent attention, five pair of eyes watched their fathers face and with what happy eyes their mother watched. Julia watched too. She could not have done otherwise if she had tried. The rain seemed to fall more gently.

Even the clock on the mantel seemed to tranquilize its tick, and on the father read. Julia thought he must have selected the longest chapter in the Bible, but none of the children complained as they knelt in prayer.

"Dear Lord," began the man. "At the end of another day, we humbly bow before Thee to thank Thee for all Thy love and mercy shown to us. We thank Thee for our home, for food and clothing, and all that makes our lives comfortable. We thank Thee for keeping us safe through the day from harm and accident and sickness. O, Lord, we thank Thee for our Church and all her activities. Help us to be true to the vows we have made to be true to our Church.

"We thank Thee for these our dear children gathered around this altar to worship Thee. O, Father, bless and keep them safe from evil and sin. Help mother and me to be the best kind of parents, to have good judgment and patience, gentleness, and love in every thing. Help us to be examples of Jesus Christ, to them in their tender years. Bless Mother in the cares and duties for tomorrow and help me too, as a husband and head of this home, to always do my duty. Be with Treva tomorrow, O God, to bless her as she goes to her place of business, to be true to Thee and let her light so shine to all those about her. Keep her from any yielding to the many temptations so many of our young girls encounter. Lord, keep her sweet and pure and true to her calling in Christ Jesus. Bless Irene tomorrow, Lord, as she goes to school. Help her in her lessons to do them thoroughly and honestly. Help her to wear the shield of faith and carry the sword of the Spirit in High School, to let her classmates know how she is a Christian and never be ashamed of our Lord and Savior Jesus Christ. O Lord, bless Henry tomorrow and help him in his peculiar temptations to be able to always say, 'I will' to the right and 'I will not' to the wrong. Keep him safe from evil company, and help him in his school work, and help him in his work after school, dear Father; keep him from any harm or danger. Bless Helen tonight, and comfort her little aching heart over the disappointment she had today. Help her to see its all for the best and help her to be a good girl tomorrow, to be obedient and kind and, Lord, give her real victories. Also, dear Lord, bless Dale tomorrow. Help him to learn to love Thee with all his heart and strength, and when he reaches the age of accountability, that he will yield his heart to Thee. Help him to overcome his temper and be obedient. And please Lord, bless little James tonight. You know that he is not very strong. O Father, if it be Thy will, give him strength and make him perfectly well again for Jesus' sake. Mother and I dedicate all of our children to Thee to be used in whatever way Thou sees fit. Make them, dear Lord, to be like Thee. Bless the visitor in our home tonight. Give her strength and courage to endure the trials she must meet every day. May she receive a blessing for being here with us in our home.

"Now, watch over us through the night; give us needed rest and peace, that we may serve Thee better tomorrow. Again, we praise Thee most precious Father, in the name of Jesus Christ. Amen."

Every one of the children from Treva to Dale, who was still awake kissed father and mother goodnight.

"Why Julia, what's the matter?"

The two girls had gone upstairs and closed the door to their room when suddenly Julia burst into tears and leaned hard against the wall and cried as though her heart were breaking.

"Why Julia dear, whatever happened?" Treva looked frightened.

"Oh it was so sweet!"

"What was so sweet?"

"The way you all gathered around together tonight and the way your father prayed for you. OH, I—"

"But we always do, like that."

"Every night, Treva?"

"Why certainly, don't you?"

"Oh no." The girl could scarcely speak. "No, no, I never heard or saw anything like that before. My mother tried to have family worship when we were little, but somehow it never worked. We tried it in the mornings, but we never could all get up before father started to work, and we just couldn't have it in the evening somehow. Everyone wanted to go to bed at a different time. Oh, Treva, I never heard my father pray for his children like that. I know he loves us and all, but, oh, how it must make you love your father!"

"It does, Julia, but he's always done like that ever since I can remember and I couldn't think of anything else."

"I can't forget it, Treva. How your little brothers and sisters pulled up their chairs and listened through all that reading! I never saw anything that made me want—want so to be better and love the Bible—and just—love everyone. Oh, it's easy to see now."

"What's easy to see?"

"Why—why more young folks don't care to come to the Bible Class and Prayer Meeting and cause so much sorry and anxiety in the Church. There are not enough family altars, Treva. I believe that's why, I really do. Nothing would seem too hard to give up or do, when you receive strength around an altar of love. If God ever gives me a home, and it has only one room, it's going to have an altar of love."

MEDITATION

By Carol Hostetler Kauffman, age 28,
Hesston College, Hesston, Kansas
Originally published June 22, 1930
in the Youth's Christian Companion

In the present day hurry and hustle, there is a serious danger of neglecting one of the most essential duties of self-development, that of quiet, serious meditation. The alarm clock always clamors mercilessly before we expect it. Breakfast is scarcely swallowed before the shop whistle blows, or the neighbor is waiting outside with his hay wagon. If we did take time for family worship, it was impossible to keep from going over (of course no one heard) the things we must do that day. And what day is there which doesn't bring us unexpected tasks, and some of those things we just had to do must be postponed until tomorrow? Very few can lay aside everything at noon to spend a few minutes in close thinking; at least not a factory employee or an office girl. Perhaps the young folks on the farm have plenty of leisure time. No? My, what a merry-go-round of a world we're living in! How many of us find time day or night to just think--just think? Those who can't sleep, wish that they could; and those who can, without any effort, wish that just once in a while they could just stay awake and think.

We are told that the bees can work best in the dark. Whether this is true or not, we can do our best thinking, when we shut out every worldly fascination, every prejudice, every unpleasant memory, and look in the realm of the beautiful. Every person should find some time every day to extract the honey-like qualities of character from life. We must begin this while we are young, while the evil days come or not; when the duties and responsibilities of life press so hard, there seems to be no more time at all for all soul-culture or spiritual brooding. Gordon said, "Youth! Thou art the time for Sediment, the time for Love, the time for Dreams, the time for Visions, the time when the Voice of Conscience is heard in the "Corridors of the Soul." Youth! The time for meditation.

Too many of us let some one else do our thinking for us and we are blindly carried away on a wave of passion or excitement. Mental sluggishness has been the curse of all ages. Meditation is the fundamental process of ways of improvement. God gave every bird its own wings with which to fly and he gave every one of us a brain with which to think, a faculty for individuality, a home within ourselves where we can go in and shut the door and kneel to our Father in secret. What a source of refreshment of spirit and what a nerving of the soul to tasks ahead! And we as young people have tasks.

How often does the God within us have a chance to visit with us? That voice is so tender, so subdued, it is not heard when we are vexed with our work, or irritated over some sore discouragement, but when we are calm of heart, even though no one praises us for the good we have done.

There have been sudden turning points in the lives of some individuals because they have employed their leisure time in serious contemplation of their own lives, their nature and dispositions, circumstances, and their own attitudes towards life. We ought to ask ourselves daily. "What am I here for anyway?" There is nothing that will act like a plow in the brain as that question. Then suddenly a star of truth from heaven shines on the soul and men and women of power step forth, for those who can face opposition foursquare and be true to the convictions within them.

Get away, if for only a few minutes each day, get away from the turmoil of business, society, and even the family, and fellowship with your own hidden self, silently, alone.

We must be governed by the Master Thinker. We must be guided by our parents, our pastor, the press, and society, but we must do our own thinking! We must know what we believe, and why, and the world ought to know it. We need young people who have the courage of their own convictions.

Meditation—what luxury! Too many of us are duplicates, far removed from originality. The greatest difference between people is not much the size of income, but the mental force. Some take time to think when others do not.

A young man living on a ranch in Colorado was startled one evening when at dusk he passed the little church-house in the valley, quarter of a mile from home, just in time to see a small slip of a figure in white open the rusty-hinged door and start in the direction of the road. The horse on which he was riding, snorted and pranced to the side of the road, then stopped. At the same instant the young man recognized the figure as his sister.

"What you doin' there Annie?"

"Oh, answered the girl shyly, "I just been where I always go after I put the turkeys in."

"But what in the world do you do in there, Annie?"

The girl's radiant face seemed transformed into one of an angel, as she stood silhouetted against the twilight sky.

"I just get better acquainted with God, Sammie, and He tells me after all, everything's going to come out all right, and it makes up for all the troubles."

There has come to my mind a legend—
A thing I half forgot,
And whether I read it or dreamed it,
Ah, well it, matters not.
It is said that in heaven at twilight
A great bell softly swings,
And man may listen and hearken

26

To the wonderful music that rings,
If he thrusts from his soul all hatred
All thoughts of wicked things,
He can hear in the holy twilight
How the bell of angels rings.
And I think there is in this legend
If we open our eyes and see,
Somewhat of an inner meaning,
My friend—to you and me.
Let us look in our hearts, and question;
'Can pure thoughts enter in
To a soul if it be already
The dwelling of thoughts of sin?'
So, then, let us ponder a little,
Let us look in our hearts, and see
If the twilight bell of angels
Could ring for you and me.

TUNING IN ON CHRISTMAS SCENES

By Christmas Carol Kauffman age 28, Hesston Kansas
Originally Published December 7, 1930
in the Youth's Christian Companion

It was the twenty-fifth of December. Yes, Christmas day! The ground was covered with a thin sheet of ice. It had been raining since dawn, a piercing, cutting, slanting rain, trying to turn into sleet any minute. It was cold and cloudy. The bare trees looked glassy. Somewhere above the trees the wind screamed and fought. Once in a while it came down and picked up every loose object, and scraped the bare, icy vines against the houses.

SCENE I.

There was a knock at the door. A middle-aged woman answered the knock. A dripping, mud-bespattered man stood at the door. He raised his hat.

"Is there a man about the place?"

"No."

"I got in the ditch down the road and thought maybe I could get a lift."

"It's too bad, but there's no man about this place."

"Well, that must be as tough as being in this ditch and a big dinner on ahead of you.

"Tough? I think I'm lucky. I pity all these women who have to fret and stew over the kitchen stove a week before Christmas and stay in bed a week after, just to please a bunch of intemperate men. Don't pity me, I'm perfectly satisfied to live alone."

"No children to gather home for Christmas?" But pardon me, I suppose you never married?"

"No, I never was married. Don't pity me. I don't have to bother about getting presents for any one. This Christmas idea is nothing but a lot of punk."

"Well, I say, you do have a gloomy idea of Christmas—and men."

"It'd be a lot better if some folks had the idea I have. Some of the neighbors round here are celebrating as though they were millionaires and can't even pay their debts. I think everyone ought to have a Christmas that suits their pocketbooks but they don't."

"People love Christmas around here and love entertaining and giving presents to each other."

"I'm glad when it's over with." She snapped. "It's stupid!

"Well, this won't get me out of the ditch. My wife and babies are getting cold. A Merry Christmas to you anyway" he said, as she shut the door with a grunt.

The man had to walk into the harsh wind as he went back toward the car. He hummed a little as he walked. It was not a real tune, however. Another traveler stopped and helped pull him out of the ditch.

"How much do I owe you my friend?"

"Your company the next three miles. I might get in you know."

"Goin home for dinner too?"

"Yes, taking the babies to see their grandma for the first time. She's been real sick to this day for over half a year now."

"Well then you can't disappoint her then. I know how they'll enjoy getting ready for us. You go ahead and I'll follow.

SCENE II.

"Turn the light on John. There, that's better. I always did like to eat Christmas dinner with the lights on. It makes it seem more special. Know what I mean? It reminds me of the Christmas dinners we used to have at the Home. How those old people did enjoy it. Take that chair there by Father. It sure seems good to have you here. I was concerned when it started to storm. I was afraid that you might not make it. Did you hear that Dave Humphrey got hurt this morning when his car jammed into the culvert?"

"No!"

"We ought to try to go over after dinner."

"Oh, thanks John."

"I haven't heard from Jim since I went away to school the first year. Does he still live with Aunt Emma?"

"I'm afraid he does. He gave his mother a beautiful purse last year, and when she showed it to me, she said nothing could have made her happier than the present of a little note, with a promise that he'd stop smoking. You could speak to Pete, Harvey, and Clinton and Evan too."

"I wonder if I could possibly locate them today since it's such weather. I know they planned on going fishing or hunting today. I'm going to try to make this an outstanding Christmas. We're supposed to give a report in Missions class in church and tell about all the opportunities we had for Christian service."

In the late afternoon John started out on his quest. Jan and woman stood at the door and watched him start out through the storm. The woman turned to her husband while tears of joy brimmed her eyes.

"If only Kizzy were living to see her boy, how grateful she would be.

30

"She doesn't have to be living Emma. She probably means more to him where he is."

"You know it seems I live all year to have that boy here over Christmas. He's such an inspiration to me. I don't care if he keeps this up all week if it means he can find these boys."

They sat for a long time thinking and watching the cold rain. The earth seemed to suck it down.

"Go along up to the attic with me Father. I'm going to get out that other woolen comforter and hunt for that essay written about "A Mother's Prayers" when John was little. I took care of John the night she read it. If I can't find it, then hopefully John will share it this Christmas.

SCENE III.

"Is Louise there?" Yes. Oh, I think it's the ugliest Christmas I have ever seen. Yes, I know. Helen Louise. How did Christmas treat you? He didn't? Oh well, it doesn't seem at all like Christmas anyway. Yes, we had turkey and all that, but it's so horrible outside. I can't bear to look out. And Uncle Harrison and family didn't get here, and we fixed for them. Now, I suppose we'll have enough leftovers to last all week. Didn't you get your watch? Oh you poor thing! That's enough to make you feel bad all year isn't it? You say Mabel got hers? Won't she be stuck up, though? Well, I'm glad I got mine for my birthday or I don't suppose I'd have gotten one either. Dad said I ought to be thankful he could get me a pair of slippers. Oh yes, pretty nice. Ann gave me a large bottle of Rose Water and I almost fell over. I just got a handkerchief for her. What did she give you? She did? What are you going to do all evening? Isn't it awful we couldn't have that sled party? It doesn't seem any more like Christmas than anything. No, there wasn't hardly anybody there. Some of the children who had pieces didn't even come. No, she didn't do good at all and she thinks she can sing so nice. Well, come over to-morrow so you can see all our presents. I've got lots to tell you. Good-bye."

SCENE IV.

How Adaline loved to say her Christmas piece! She had given it that evening before, so sweet, half shy, and graceful. Every person in the audience bent forward in eager admiration. The child's voice was delicate but clear.

"Mother," the child called and came bounding.

"Yes, dear."

"I want to speak my piece again."

"All right, Adaline dear."

"Let's play church. We'll play this is the platform. Daddy, you and mother listen." She stood up on her play box.

> "Why do bells at Christmas ring?
> Why do little children sing?
> Oh, because a Babe once lay
> Pillowed soft upon the hay.
> And its mother sang and smiled.
> This is Christ the Holy Child."

The doorbell rang. The neighbors had come over to spend the evening. They had a child the same age as Adaline.

"Oh, I'm so glad you came. Let's play church and say our pieces."

"No."

"Yes, let's do. I like mine so."

"No."

"Don't you like yours?"

"No,"

"Don't you like to say yours to your mother and daddy?"

"No"

"Why?"

"Cause."

"Why not?"

"It really isn't true."

"What isn't true?"

"Daddy don't love Jesus and me like my piece says he does, and Mamma cries when I say it."

Adaline ran to the child's father and looked up into his face. He had not heard the childish conversation.

"Don't you love Jesus?"

"Why—a—what's—this, Adaline?"

"Like Josie's piece says."

"I—I—" He tried to evade the child's questions and enter into another conversation, but she would not be evaded. No one could evade Adaline.

"Why does it make her cry?" She pointed to the child's mother.

A deadly silence fell on the group. Adaline's mother caught her breath. Her child, her own little Adaline! What should she say? She must say something, but what?

The man crossed the room and took the child in his arms—his child.

"By God's help, Josie, little girl, it shall never make your mamma cry again. We're going to have Christmas every day now.

SCENE V.

Georgie lay in the hospital flat on his back. Several persons had been to see him, but still he watched the door eagerly. Was it really Christmas?

"She will surely come yet." He said to himself.

Every footstep made his heart jump. Georgie was ten but his heart felt so big. Many things had happened to make it feel so. He had been sick for eight long months. Blood poison had set in from a little bruise on the foot. The doctor had said he could not get well. Georgie did not know it but she did. Georgie would not have objected had they told him. A child could not have suffered more than he had.

"It must be eight o'clock. Surely she will come yet."

She did come finally. She was tall, and wore a plain black coat.

"Well, Georgie, how are you?"

She bent over and kissed his cheek.

"Oh, Grandma, I thought you'd never come, but yet I knew you would."

"I know, Georgie, but the train was late, that's why. Was your mother in to see you?"

The boy shook his head. "Uncle Joe was here and brought me that candy, but I can't eat it. Martha gave me that book. I wanted a Bible so much."

"Bless your heart, child, that's what I brought you." She handed him the beautiful black book. He took it and pressed it to his lips.

"Oh, Grandma, how I love it!"

Was this a boy or an angel in disguise? The woman sat and looked at the child's pale face. The child, her own daughter's boy, abused, and shamefully mistreated. She was probably at a dance in some neighboring town, and hadn't even been in to see her child on Christmas.

"Oh, God, why do you tolerate such things?

"Why? Why must he suffer so? Why are not our prayers answered? Georgie's and mine? Where is his father tonight? And Elva? How can a mother be so cruel-hearted? Why was Georgie always hated? He had never been a mean child. Why couldn't he die? Poor boy, poor child!"

On and on the woman thought and hot tears rolled down her cheeks. Still Georgie lay with his eyes closed. Was he going?"

"Georgie?"

"Yes Grandma."

"Were you—sleeping dear?"

"No, I was praying. What were you praying, Georgie?"

"I want so to get well, Grandma, and be a preacher."

"Yes, Goergie," was all she said. *What if he knew what the Doctor said?*

"I feel like I'd like to go to heaven, Georgie—I do often."

"Heaven? Yes, I'd rather do that, too, and I thought I could to-day, but I couldn't until you came."

A strange fear seized hold of the woman. What if he should die? Her little Georgie! He was the child she had prayed for and tired to protect all his life, her only friend in the family. Perhaps that's why they hated her so. She loved him. They both loved God. How they loved Him!

The sound of voices, oh, so clear and sweet, wafted inward from the hall. A group of Christmas carolers had stopped on the third landing. Georgie pressed his Bible closer and smiled. It was like the dawn of a summer morning lighting up his face. "Do you hear the music Georgie?" She whispered? He did not answer. She touched him but he did not respond.

"Oh Georgie, Georgie—has your eternal Christmas come at last?" Lord, can't I go along with my little Georgie?"

BERNARD'S GRANDY

By Christmas Carol Kauffman, age 29, Hesston, Kansas
Originally published January 11, 1931
in the Youth's Christian Companion

Bernard called the old man Grandy, and Grandy's plump, rosy-faced wife, Brandy. He called them that from the beginning. No one had attempted any suggestion of such titles, but they simply gushed out of Bernard's mouth unconsciously, and the old couple never objected, not once.

They had no grandchildren of their own, but Mollie Graham had many a grandmotherly way about her, and Mose had many a grandfatherly way about him too; the right vest pocket for peppermints, the hearty laugh, and tender voice, and a mind brim full of juvenile rhymes. No wonder the children never hesitated to "make up" with Mose Graham, and little wonder that Bernard named him Grandy.

It happened one day after Mollie Graham answered a hesitant, almost fearful knock at the side door. There stood a dispirited, forlorn-looking boy in clothes as wretched as his blue face and hands.

"Do you want to buy a rose?" He asked in a voice even more pitiful, and he held out one poorly made paper one.

Mollie didn't want an imitation in her house, not even in the attic, and she knew it, but she asked the price in the kindest motherly voice. That was like Mollie Graham.

"Ten cents," he answered between his chattering teeth.

"You poor child, you're nearly frozen, aren't you? Come inside and get warm." He did not have to be coaxed.

"Here, child, stand on this register. Don't you go to school?

"Yes'um, when I'm home."

"Where do you live?"

"In Oklahoma."

"Oklahoma? Are you here alone?"

"No'm." He kept his eyes on the floor, and the corners of his mouth twitched. Mollie noticed it.

"Did you move here?"

"Huh-hu."

"How long have you been here?"

"Three days."

"Where are your mother and father?"

"I don't know. My uncle's down there in one of those cabins." The boy looked up almost hopelessly, and moved toward the door.

"Do they sell them too?"

He shook his head.

"Did you sell many today?"

"Nah, never do."

The boy turned his head, but not so quickly that Millie did not see that he brushed away a tear with his jacket sleeve.

"Don't you have an overcoat, child?"

He shook his head.

"Don't you get an awful cold?"

He nodded.

"Are you hungry?"

He nodded again.

Just then Mose came in the back door, and before coming into the next room said, "Mollie, I smell something mighty appetizing. Whew, an' fresh bread too—eh? Who's this now?"

"Mose, it's a perfect shame this child has to tramp the streets, and try to sell those flowers. And with no overcoat, and as cold as it is! He ought to be in school." She was almost cross.

"I declare," said Mose. "How old are you, boy?"

"Eight."

"Don't the truant officers get after you?"

"We keep movin all the time."

"What's tha—" but Mollie cut him short, and answered the question for the boy. The child worked closer to the door. His dirty hand was on the knob. He must go! He feared this woman the old man called Millie, yet it was so cozy inside, and her voice was not desperate because of anything he had done. The odor from the kitchen made him weak. He must go! But Mollie kept on talking. He could not understand all she was saying and it frightened him. He opened the door and ran down the steps, forgetting the rose on the chair. She came to the door and called, "Come back dear boy and have some dinner!"

"Can't, they'll get after me."

"Come on", demanded Mose, in a compassionate voice, the boy absolutely could not, but obeyed.

Oh my! How he ate. Color came to his face. And his eyes lost their wistful, mischievous stare.

"By chance is your name Bernard?"

"Yes'um."

"Bernard what?" asked Mose.

"Bernard Tucker."

"Well, now Bernard," began Mose, after he had finished the piece of pumpkin pie. I'm going down the street with you and I want you to show me where you are staying, because I want to talk to your uncle."

"About what?" a terrified look seized his face. He clutched at his jacket.

"Don't worry son."

Neither spoke another word until they neared the cabin at the end of the village. The young boy stopped short and caught his breath.

"The rose, the rose!" The boy caught his breath again. I forgot—and left it—back at the – oh he will for sure strap me!" Huge tears welled up in the boy's eyes and he bit his fingers in fear. The tears seemed to freeze in his eyes because it was oh, so cold!

"How much was it?" asked Mose as he reached in his pocket.

"Ten cents, but she didn't say she wanted one!"

"Please, I want it" And he handed the forlorn, scared child a dime.

No one answered Mose's rap, but he heard voices inside the room as they stood near the door.

A woman in soiled knickers stepped aside and gave Mose a questioning look, and spoke not a word.

"Howdy do," ventured Mose as he tilted his hat.

"Howdy do," she answered without approaching the door. She did not smile in the least. The boy who had been kept inside received an almost wicked look. Mose could see the young boy tremble.

"I have come here to talk to you about your boy."

"What about our boy?" Demanded an ugly voice from a man with a three days growth of whiskers on his dirty face. He stepped out from behind the door.

"He stopped at our house to—"

"Well, what of that!"

"It's alright if it's during the day."

"Not unless the boy is physically disabled, am I obligated by law to keep him inside during the day."

"And what authority do you have to come here and warn me of that! Don't you think I know?"

He took a step closer to Mose and clenched his fists in his pockets. The woman stepped up indigently and started to say something, but the man waved her silent.

"I don't know if you know it or not, but the boy is not mentally sick!"

"This young boy is physically disabled and should not be alone in the streets without a responsible adult by his side."

"Is that so?! Well, our son is excused from school because of a physical condition, and would you please go along and mind your own business!" The man's eyes became slits, and his breath hissed from between his teeth. Mose did not move.

"If you can show me your written permit of exemption I will leave you in peace. And, by the way, the boy says you are not his father, and he does not know where his parents are." Mose spoke in a firm, steady voice, and his gray hair, and fixed blue eyes, only added more dignity to his character, and the man in front of him, though much larger in size, seemed to cower or shrink before him. His uncle's face grew red, and the veins in his neck beat irregularly above his collar. He cleared his throat to speak, but did not. Mose calmly drew his watch from his pocket, glanced at it, and replaced it.

"I will show it only if I care to." The man's voice was a trifle unsteady.

"Very well, you must let me see it!"

The man did not move. The moment that followed was tense, not for Mose, but for the other one. He swallowed saliva in great gulps. The woman pinched her arms nervously. Bernard only stared in fearful alarm.

"I shall lose no time in reporting you." Mose did not snap the words.

The man made no answer. His face grew pale under his whiskers, and the woman grew whiter. Fully a minute passed, still not a word.

"I tell you," said Mose at last, "You can let the boy go with me, or be reported at once." And the man knew that Mose meant what he said.

"Take him", bawled out the man. "Take him," said the woman at the very same time, waving her arms in the air. "Goodness knows he's made us trouble enough already."

"Come Bernard," said Mose, and without another word he took the boy's hand and left the cabin. Not another word! Not a good bye! Not one backward look from the boy!

In the distance from the cabin to the Graham house Bernard learned to trust Mose. Not once did his step lag. Not once did he show fear, except when he heard footsteps coming. He turned around sharply and grasped Mose's hand. It was only the milkman.

What did Mollie say? She put her arms around the boy's shoulders, and gave Mose the fondest look she had given him since the day he brought in the white pine chest he made in the woodshed. Not a great many women were as kindly uncritical as Mollie Graham.

An hour later when Mollie sent Mose back to the cabin to get the boy's clothes (the boy said he had a few) the occupants had left, and upon inquiry, the cabin owner told Mose they had left at least there-quarters of an hour ago. Mose did not care much.

And Bernard called Mose Grandy from the beginning and Mollie Granny.

The first night, when Millie sent Mose to the room with a cup of hot chocolate for Bernard ("so's he can go right off to sleep" as she put it) he looked up into his face and said, "Oh, you're jus' grandy, grand to me!"

About a month later Mose said to Millie as he helped her put her quilt frame, "Yes, we are getting pretty old, I know. And maybe he would get better training in a Home. In a year or so John wonders if we can manage him. And he'll cost us more all the time."

"I don't know what to do, Mose. I hardly see how we can keep him for good, much as we think of him."

"The door opened and in ran Bernard all out of breath. "Oh, Grandy," He cried in a strange excitement. "God did find me you, didn't He?"

"Why, yes, Bernard."

"And He will let me stay here always, won't He?"

"Why, yes, Bernard."

"Jimmy Hensol said maybe I couldn't and his father said God isn't nobody and don't know nothing."

"Well, you tell Jimmy I said, God knows even what people think, and how to find homes for boys, and you can stay here as long as you're a good boy."

"Oh, I'll be good, Grandy. You jes' make me be."

DALE'S DIARY

By Christmas Carol Kauffman, age 29, Hesston, Kansas
Originally published March 1, 1931
in the Youth's Christian Companion

Mar 2

Uncle Ben left today on the 9:10 train. These were the best revival meetings we've ever had. Everybody says so. He got $62.00. That's pretty good for our congregation and lots of folks out of work. I'm glad I gave that dollar I was going to buy that saw with 'cause Pa found one today. I made two more new drawings for my birdhouses. I can hardly wait till I get started. I want to make at least one every evening this month, then start peddling. I don't want any of the fellows to find it out or they'd start it too, or laugh at me for investing my 50 cents this way.

Mar 3

We sure do miss Uncle Ben at the breakfast table and Ma doesn't bother often to make waffles unless there's company. Ma told me to throw the dresser scarf in his room down the clothes shoot, and I found a card under it. I don't know whether it was sent it to him or not. I don't know who else it might belong to, yet it can hardly be his. He is almost perfect. I will keep it in my diary anyway. No, I will copy it. It can't be Uncle Ben's. There are some things I need to be doing better at. Here is my list I am making today.

     1. I must think twice before I speak.
     2. I must keep every friend I make.

3. I must show more appreciation.
4. I must not neglect the children.
5. I must save every cent I can.
6. I must expect less of others and more of myself.
7. I must do away with pride.
8. I must never complain.
9. I must have more faith.
10. I must pray more, more, more!
   God help me!

Mar 4

Ted's dad said he can't go skating unless some man's along, so Mr. Berman took our whole class out to Pine Creek tonight. There wasn't any Prayer Meeting on account of the smallpox quarantine. Clausens have it now. Mr. Berman said the best preventative is to get plenty of out-door exercise, and rest. Ma wasn't just awful anxious for me to go. I could tell, but she didn't say so. She can't forget the time when she went through the ice when she was a girl. Well, we picked out a shallow place on purpose, and say, we had fun, only it lasted only about an hour. Ma had chili soup and fresh buns for supper.

Mar 5

They closed school to fumigate; and we have to get vaccinated. Our meetings closed just in time. I finished one birdhouse all except the painting. It doesn't go as fast as I thought it would. Martha thinks she has to watch me every now and then, and it bothers a fellow.

Mar 6

I made two houses today and started a third one. I think they're nifty. Martha said it hurts to get vaccinated, but I thought it was fun. School may open Monday; I hope not. I think I can ask $1.00 a piece for the hinged bottom Blue Bird houses, and the Robin roosts, and the Wren houses, and maybe $2.00 for the Martin. I don't know yet. I wonder if any of the other fellows invested quarters this way. I think when I 'm through school, I'll go into the business and make pergolas and garden seats, trellises and so forth. I'd rather make bird-houses than go skating.

Mar 7

Tim is still a few points ahead of me in our contest. He had a letter from China today and I had some reports from the Missionary Review. That's the first letter anybody's had yet from China. George says he's getting tired writing letters. Ma has given me 14 stamps so far. Seven more Sundays and we'll know who wins. I used to think Tim tried so hard just to get that Bible, but I really believe he's going to be a missionary himself some day. Aunt Susie was here for dinner.

Mar 8

I sure think I'm lucky. I can get all the boxes I need for my houses at Zint's Grocery and I got the paint and hinges at Browns for 50 cents, and Pa said if I need any more hinges or nails he'll donate them. A fellow in the country can raise a calf or a pig or something, but us city fellows have to use our heads. School may open Wed. I hope not.

Mar 9

I've been wondering about something all day. Did Uncle Ben put that card under the dresser scarf? Is it his, and why did he write it, if he did? I never thought he was proud a bit, and I never heard him complain or forget to say thanks or anything. If a minister like Uncle Ben needs to say thanks or anything. If a minister like Uncle Ben needs to write all that, I ought to start one with fifty points. I said something today I wouldn't have said if I had thought twice.

Mar 10

Mrs. Henderson came over to spend the day and she offered to iron for Ma while Ma got the dinner and ironing board collapsed and nearly smashed her big toe, so Pa had to take her home right away. Ma felt so bad over it she couldn't eat any dinner, then Pa and I each got an extra custard. It's been snowing all afternoon and it looks like a blizzard is beginning to start.

Mar 11

The snow was four feet deep beside our house this morning. The paper tonight says they will pay shovelers 23 cents an hour over in the Ramford Place. I'm going over at 6:30 AM. Parkie is gong with me. The Walkover Shoe Store in town is gave away a pair of shoes to the boy or girl that could get the most words out of "Walkover Shoes," and Parkie got them. His list will be in tomorrow's paper. He said no one helped him either.

Mar 12

School will be open tomorrow. Martha imagines she is getting the pox. Oh, I hope not! I made $1.25 shoveling snow today. I'm sure tired. We got a letter from Uncle Ben today and he asked if we got the 'reminder sheet". He said he was checking himself over after and put it over on the dresser and couldn't find it in the morning. I s'pect we got it under the cover and didn't know it. Then Ma wondered if I saw it and why I never said anything about it. I went upstairs and got it out of this book, and Ma and Pa said her brother always did write down such things, and he was always the best in the family. They talked mostly about Uncle Ben saying he had to save every cent he could. Martha and I sat and listened.

Mar 13

They had a health officer talk to us in the gym this morning. He sent nine home and said they had to have their tonsils out or their ears fixed or something like that. He poked around in my throat and said, "Pass on—next." I wish it was warmer up here in my room so I could read "Hannington." I like to be alone when I read it. I found a dime on the railroad crossing. Lucky, huh!

Mar 14

I worked most all day on Wren houses. After this snow melts, I will be even more enthusiastic. It seemed like ten miles around my paper route tonight and about half my customers said, "I'll try to pay next Saturday." I'm sure glad I have a letter to read tomorrow. All us fellows like Mr. Berman better all the time. I like the way he walks and like the way he runs his hand through his hair. I hope when I'm 21, Pa will get me a watch like he's got.

Mar 15

There were only 41 in Sunday School, so we all stayed upstairs and had the lesson all together. Mr. Kerr talked mostly to the children and the big folks acted more interested than when they go to their classes, Pa said. They make long prayers for the sick and depressed and out of work. I pray every day that Pa won't get laid off. Ma said if he was, we have to live on mush and milk and only burn enough coal to heat one room. I'm sure they couldn't get along without Pa working.

Mar 16

It's warmer today. I have twelve houses finished. If I were a bird I would nest in one. Ma said folks won't have money for such things as bird houses. The folks I go to will.

Mar 17

Ma is helping me plan the best surprise for Mr. Berman's birthday. It's going to be here on Tuesday night. I must tell all the fellows tomorrow. Ma called up most of the guys mothers today. Ma suggested it. I'm glad.

Mar 18

The Prayer Meeting was good but it made me feel like a grain of salt. They talked about the do's and the don'ts of a Christian. There's more things that I don't do than I do. I'm glad no one else can tell what a fellow is thinking of. Sometimes I have a big notion to burn this. I don't think any of the other fellows keep a diary, but I must appreciate Aunt Fanny's present, Ma says. She said I'll be glad some day that I kept one up.

Mar 19

He sure was surprised! Ma is a dear, but I didn't have the nerve to tell her. We each gave a dime and got him a little notebook. We had sandwiches and pickles and apple pie. Ma had some homemade games made out and Pa helped to play, too. Martha said we made more noise than 23 girls would, but I objected. Mr. Berman is 31. Ma said she wonders why he never got married yet.

Mar 20

I was called to the desk today for whispering. When a girl asks a fellow a question twice he can't set there like a hall tree. Since it was Mary Ann, I didn't tell on her. Henry asked me today how come I don't believe in smoking. We had a regular debate, but Tom said I won. They always pick on me to spring a question. Tim says if I keep on, I'll be a preacher some day.

Mar 21

I worked all day collecting like we were poor.

Mar 22

I have a notion to write a list of reminders like Uncle Ben does. This is just between us three, God-me- and my diary. It might help me do better if I read these everyday from now on.

1. I must quit running with Harry.

2. I must speak to folks on the street.
3. I must make more birdhouses before spring.
4. I must clean my fingernails before Ma has to tell me.
5. I must get my lessons better.
6. I must stop teasing Martha about her freckles.
7. I must try to take smaller bites.
8. I must get up when Ma calls me.
9. I must start a record of expenses and earnings.
10. I must put the papers up to the door.
11. I must try to like Miss Stevenson.
12. I must carry out the ashes before Pa makes me.
13. I must say, "Pardon" me more.
14. I must add to this list as I need.

ALYCE JEAN'S MONOLOGUE

By Christmas Carol Kauffman, age 29, Hesston, Kansas
Originally published March 8, 1931
in the Youth's Christian Companion

Move over a little Lula; you're right in the middle of the bed. Wait—don't take all the cover with you. Oh, I forgot I'm going to fix a cord on this light tomorrow and tie it over here on the head of the bed, then I can turn it out after I'm in. I know I'm cold. My feet are just—Lula! Don't yell like that; you'll wake up the folks. Oh, about nine-thirty. No, I came straight home. Yes, I locked the door. They were all there but Mabel. I don't know. I suppose her Dad wouldn't let her. Well, he never does let her go to any of our class doings. I guess it's because Mrs. Kimble is our teacher. I don't know, only that's what Mrs. Kimble said. Don't you remember? Sure you do. How Mrs. Kimble sent him that "Anti-Tobacco" paper and he got so furious? Why, I knew you knew it. Well, I don't either but he did, and tries to show his spite by making Mabel stay at home every time we want to have an extra special meeting.

Yes, we finished it! I never saw a bunch of girls work so fast and talk so little. Well, Lula we did tonight anyway. Part of the time it was perfectly quiet. We had to finish it tonight so we could send it along with Smiths in the morning. Are you asleep Lula? Didn't you hear Mamma say they were going to Canada for two weeks? She told us at the breakfast table. You must have had your mind some other place. He's going on business about this Russian relief work. I don't know. Mrs. Smith has relatives there. That doesn't make any difference. Mrs. Smith said their church was sewing for them, too, and she'd see that it was given to the right persons. Oh, not exactly pretty, but it'll be good and warm anyway. They'll be glad for it. They won't care if it is made of all shapes and sizes. It's thick and soft. We had enough but one little piece, and I cut a piece out of my inner coat lining. I did Lula! Oh, just a piece about three inches square. No one will ever know the difference. Well, if Mamma knew how much we needed it just then she'd never say a word. No it won't. You couldn't find the place I'll bet.

I heard something tonight I'll tell you tomorrow. I want to go to sleep now. I'll tell you tomorrow. Yes, you can wait. Yes, you can. You couldn't guess all night. No, Elisabeth told me. Tonight. She said she knew it for a long time. Go to sleep. Well, I am though. Yes, it sure is something nice. It would take too long. Oh, Lula don't get so excited. Well, you're awful inquisitive then. What? No, I'm not teasing.

O well, it's just that John—Well, give me a chance to sneeze. Lula let me put my feet against yours. John's going away to school next week. Virginia. He doesn't have any, but some friend of his is going to send him. Why, a man who lives in that flat where he fires. That's part you never could guess, Lula. Yes, my feet are warmer. You know he goes down there to take care of the furnace three times a day, and goes back again in the evening since it's so cold? Well, one evening he met two fellows about sixteen years old, standing on the corner just tipsy enough they didn't know just where they were. He took them along down to the basement with him and talked to them a long time. The next evening they came back again, and had another boy with them. And Elizabeth said those boys got so interested in what John had to tell them, that they met John down there several times every week. Yes. Why he talked to them about the Bible, and they formed some kind of a class. Didn't you see those three strange boys with John the last few Sunday evenings? Yes. But listen Lula, no one knew a thing about it, but I forgot the man's name. He lives in the flat, and was down in the basement one evening, in the next room, or some place Elizabeth didn't just say, but anyway, he heard the boys talk and since then this old man has talked a lot to John and he's going to send him to school to prepare for the ministry. I don't know. John's folks didn't know he was doing it until this man made the offer to him. Sure, he's a Christian. I think Elizabeth said he belongs to the Brethren Church. Anyway, isn't it the most wonderful thing you ever heard of? Huh? What's the matter? Lula, you're crying! I know it. I never heard anything that made me feel so—so worthless. Why, because I never did anything—anything at all. Oh, John he's— Yes you said it—just wonderful! I always knew he'd surprise us all some day. By Sunday everyone will know it. Yes, he's leaving next week. Why Lula, don't take it like that! What? You're going to get out and pray. I'm coming with you. Lula don't cry so. You—you make me—Oh, Lula I want to do something like that too.

IN THE TIME OF LILACS

By Christmas Carol Kauffman, age 29, Hesston, Kansas
Originally published April 12, 19 and 26, 1931
in the Youth's Christian Companion

The large awkward looking house on the hill at the end of Mason Street was known throughout the town as the Old Lilac Place. Years ago the people who had erected the then magnificent structure had planted a hedge of lilac bushes around the entire lot. In the spring of the year it was a sight worth walking out of one's way to see. It certainly was. From the bottom of the hill the blossom-covered bushes made a wondrous splash of beauty against the sunset sky and the house seemed to be folded in the arms of flower land. Many evening strollers chose Mason Street to see the Lilac Place, where they paused to touch the plumb, waxy petals, or bury their faces in them to take in their perfume. Children tripped by, and irresistibly broke off some of the outward-leaning sprays. Lovers lingered a moment in the cool of the evening to whisper the sweet story of love.

But that was years ago. Not many people went out of their way any more to see the Old Lilac Place. It was in a sorely dilapidated condition now. Many of the bushes were stubbed off and scrawny, and some were missing altogether. A number of the balusters in the long side porch were missing too. The paint was so badly faded, it might have been either green or blue. Many families had moved in and left again.

The house had been empty for some time, just before the Carringtons came. The neighbors all rejoiced at their coming; of course not to the family directly, at least not many, but they did among themselves. Anyone would rather look up the street to lighted windows than dark ones.

There were four in the family. The little girl was eight or nine. One can't judge by size, but she was just tall enough to reach into the mailbox if she stood on her tiptoes. Her face was pale and her light hair hung in straggly curls around her face. While the other children in the neighborhood ran and squealed and played, the little girl sat on the porch steps, bending over a book in her lap.

An elderly lady was frequently seen about the house. Her step was short and quick and she seemed to have the responsibility of the household while the child's mother was away. Every day the mother went early and returned late. So did the father.

One beautiful Saturday morning, about two weeks after the coming of this family to the neighborhood, a young woman started up the hill toward the Lilac Place. She carried a leather bag and a bunch of cards in her hand. Some kind of an agent, no doubt, for she stopped at every house. Some asked her in, some didn't.

She glanced at her watch. It was ten of four. The walk leading to the end of the street was rough and broken. Several times she halted as if between two opinions—go back or on. She kept on. There was one more house before the Lilac Place.

As she was leaving that house the woman called out, "Say, Lady, there's someone living up there in the Old Lilac Place again."

"Really?"

"Yes. They moved in a couple of weeks ago. I thought I'd tell you."

"Thank you. I was wondering whether it was worth while to climb the hill."

Halfway up the hill the young woman noticed curtains at the windows. As she turned at the hedge entrance, she saw a child in blue gingham sitting on the steps, intent on something

55

in her lap. The child did not look up until the woman called out, "Hello, little girl!"

Instantly the child got to her feet, and, closing the book with her finger inserted to mark the place, smiled and answered the greeting. Her big gray eyes opened wide and she looked at the woman questioningly.

"Is your mother at home?"

"No."

"She isn't?"

"No. She's never home days, you know."

"I see. I suppose she works."

"Yes, she's a bookkeeper at Penner's"

"Well, I think you can answer my question then." The woman took her pencil and copied the number of the house.

"And what is your father's name." The woman's kind smile brought forth a yet kinder one from the child. Her voice was delicate and clear.

"Frank Carrington."

"How many children in the family?"

"Oh, I'm the only child we've got. Billie, he died before I was born, and Mother and Father were so forsaken until I came. I'd love to have a sister, but Father says I'm all he can handle; but I'd do the taking care of her.

The woman smiled. The child went on.

"Mother and Father are working to pay for grandpa's funeral and all, you know. It cost tremendously, Mother said. That's why we moved up here, you know. It's so much cheaper."

"I see," said the woman. "I didn't know any one was living here until I stopped down the street. I was told someone moved in. The house was empty the last time I passed."

"We've been living here for two weeks now. It will be two weeks tomorrow. My, the house was so dirty and dusty. Mother had a notion not to stay, but we did anyway."

The child gave her head a little jerk sideways and pranced from one step to the other.

"Do you like it here?"

"Oh, yes. I do, but Mother doesn't. But I sure do. The house is so big and romantic, and full of corners and so many doors. It keeps me guessing where they all lead to, but I've got it all learned now. And I like this long porch, and the bushes. I suppose they'll be real pretty when they once come out."

"I know they used to be beautiful."

"That's what Mother said. We used to live down on the edge of the marsh. It was a real cute house, a bungalow, you know; but I always did want to live up on a hill. It's so sophisticated, you know, to pretend it's a palace or a castle."

The child's eyes danced and her face was alive with expression. A surprised, half-amused look crossed the woman's face. She studied the child, as some do a bit of spicy gossip.

"What's your name, my child?"

"Josie."

"Josie?"

"Josie Dell Carrington. I'm named after my two grandmothers," she said proudly.

"And how old are you, Josie?"

"Eight. Well, nearly nine, but—but I'm eight now."

"And what's that you've been reading?"

"The House Of Seven Gables."

The young woman was quite taken back.

"And—and—you really like it?" She asked with surprise.

"Sure I do. Phoebe is so clever and Hepzibah so quaint." Josie opened the book admiringly.

"But don't you have any books for little girls to read. Why, that's a book for high school pupils."

"Well, I found it in the bookcase. I've read all the books but two. Let's see, 'Tales From Shakespeare' and ' Select Orations.' I will read them next.

"Dear me," said the woman surprisingly. That's a shame. You ought to have books to read that were written especially for girls like you. Do you have any good Bible story books?"

"No, we never—" she shook her head.

"Well, I'm out helping to canvas the neighborhood. We're taking the religious census and finding out how many boys and girls go to Sunday School and how many don't.

"You never go anywhere?"

"Not any more. I used to a long time ago, but it's so long I can't hardly remember."

"Why did you stop going?"

"Oh, you see, Mother is always so tired on Sundays; so we all sleep till noon; only I don't. I keep a book under my pillow. I just can't keep my eyes open after seven-thirty." She took a deep breath.

"Wouldn't you like to start going to Sunday School again?" She nodded most earnestly.

"Our Church is only four blocks down the street. We'd love to have you come tomorrow and see how you like it. And you could bring home the nicest books from the library every Sunday. We have books for girls just your age, Josie."

"Do they really and they wouldn't cost me anything?"

"They wouldn't cost you a cent; and a little girl as smart as you could get up and get herself ready, don't you think?"

"Oh yes, I always do. I can do anything like that!"

"I thought you could. Who taught you to read?"

"I don't know, I guess I just always knew how."

The census lady smiled. Josie flew down the steps like a bird and looked up into her face.

"Oh, she cried, you must be even prettier than Violetta in the Poet's Garden. She had only one dimple and I don't think she had a gold tooth on the side like that."

The woman blushed and laughed and gave Josie a little pat on the cheek. Very, very few people had paid her such a compliment. It fell into her heart and lodged there. It struck a spot not many children had discovered, for she was not the kind of a woman to love all children. Even though she had been a Sunday School teacher from her teens, she somehow did not possess the backward, the ugly-duckling kind as well as the sweet. She would hardly have fitted in as a worker in a children's home. Some children flocked around her and others shrank, not knowing what it was or wasn't about her that caused the children to do so.

Suddenly she grew to love Josie Carrington. She was a dear, sweet child, and pretty too. Yes, she was. Aren't children pretty and sweet if their noses are short and hair a faded straw color?

"When I'm as big as you, I hope I can have a gold tooth too! Are they very expensive?"
Josie touched the woman's dress.

"Quite expensive." And the woman gave her another pat on the cheek.

"I don't suppose your mother and father go to church and hold their membership anywhere?" she continued, filling out the card.

"No, just at the Lodge. Father says all the churches just want his money."

"Shall I look for you tomorrow at nine thirty?"

"Would you be my teacher?"

"Yes, and there are nine other little girls just your age!"

"Oh, if you will really be my teacher, then I think I will come. I'll try anyway. Will you meet me at the door?"

"I'll try to Josie. If I'm not there just go and sit with all the other girls who are just your age. My name is Ella Simmons."

"Ella Simmons; I won't forget. I will just ask for the lady with the dimples and go."

"I'll be there, Josie."

"Josie—Josieeeee!" called a shrill voice from the house.

"Yes, Grandma, I'm coming."

"It's about time you're coming, Josie. Are you reading so hard again you can't hear when I call?"

"Why, I came right exactly the first time I heard you, Grandma. Honest!"

"What are you doing? Reading?"

"No, I was talking to a lady, a Sunday School census lady."

"What do you mean?"

"Well, you know, Grandma, to find out how many little boys and girls go to Sunday School and who don't. And just think Grandma, if I go I can bring home library books, free, and written especially just for me!"

"Well, what I know is that they may be better for you than the kind you are reading. I think it high time you're starting to Sunday School before you get as careless as your mother and father are."

"Why don't you go to, Grandma?"

"Fetch me in some water this minute!"

"Do you think I can go, Grandma?"

"Where?"

"To Sunday School."

"Yes."

Josie left for the water and came back all breathless and flushed.

"Do you, Grandma? I could get up by myself and get ready and not need to wake up Mother and Father."

"I suppose you could."

The old woman hummed a little as she went about to work. She thought of the time she tried to climb up into the old surrey and sit beside her father as they drove off to the little church by the timberline. She wore her oiled boots and her pink sunbonnet. Those were happy days. The father wasn't a church member, but he saw to it that the children went to church, rain or shine. But somewhere along the way, he dropped out, and never had gone back again. She never went to church anymore except for funerals. No, Maggie Carrington didn't go to church, but that's not saying she didn't want little Josie to go.

***

The lilac hedge was in its earliest buds in the morning. Josie spied one half-open cluster on the south side. She carried it in her hand as she went down the hill while Grandmother watched her from the window.

Ella Simmons was there to meet her, sure enough, and accepted the lilac spray with a hearty thank you.

Josie wore a green chambray jumper dress, with an ill-made blouse of some cheap white material. Her curls were still damp. Some of the ill-mannered children stared at her curiously, and whispered among themselves. Did Josie notice it? She did. And under her little white blouse, something like a pinching pain worked. The children looked just as strange to her, as she did to them. But Ella Simmons was so nice to her, and the story she told was every bit as interesting as "House Of Seven Gables." Before she knew it she was leaning forward in her chair. She watched. She listened. She hungrily absorbed it all.

"Is it a real true story?" She asked, "or is it a make-believe kind?"

Some of the girls snickered; some stared. Miss Simmons frowned.

"That really happened, Josie," said the teacher, giving the girls who laughed a helpless look. "And if you come every Sunday you will hear many more."

In the next six months which followed, Josie missed but one Sunday. And only on that one Sunday did she miss taking home two beloved library books. Oh, how she loved those books. And they must have loved her too. She just knew they did, for they told her such new happy stories. The characters talked right to Josie. Shy, they seemed to know her, even the language they thought. In their rich, simple language they spread over her heart like a fire across a prairie. Sometimes they shone like a bright star far up in the heavens on a dark night. She lived in those books.

"Brother Gowen," said Ella Simmons one Sunday. "I want to speak to you about one of my pupils, Josie Carrington."

"Yes."

"I suppose you have noticed her."

"That little pale-faced—"

"Yes. That's Josie. She is a very remarkable child, Brother Gowen."

"So I've been told."

"She knew practically nothing of the Bible when she came, but in less than a year now she has advanced beyond the rest of the class."

"I'm glad to hear it, Ella."

"And I believe with a little encouragement she would be willing to enter the class with the other converts, and be ready for baptism by Christmas. I thought I'd mention it to you, and you can do as you see fit."

"Have you ever spoken to her about it?"

"No, I haven't, Brother Gowen. I don't ever rush the children you know."

"Yes," was all he said.

"I thought if you talked with her you could tell better, you know."

"I'll do that, Ella. Let me see, she lives—"

"At the Old Lilac Place."

"Beg your pardon?"

"At the Old Lilac Place, at the end of Mason."

"Oh, yes."

The following Wednesday at four o'clock the minister started up the hill. The bright October sun was still warm, and the flutter of gently falling leaves added more character to the day. Josie was sitting at her favorite spot reading. She did not notice the minister until he was almost to the steps.

"So this is where you live, Josie?"

The minister was a well-built medium sized man with an extra amount of heavens light on his face. His voice was deep and kind. He took Josie's hand and held it tenderly. When she looked up at him he saw that she was a child of unusual personality.

"May I sit here on the steps beside you?" She moved over.

"I just love it here. I do not know what I will do when I can't sit out here in the winter."

"You'll just be that happier to see spring come then."

"Why, you're like Pollyanna, aren't you?"

"Not so much as I ought to be, Josie." "I came," said the minister, "to ask you how you like Sunday School by this time."

The child's face darkened and she turned her head and half closed her eyes.

"You like it pretty well, don't you?" he asked.

"Well, well, not as well as I did."

"What?" He turned abruptly. The child made no answer, but fumbled with the pages of her book. Her cheeks grew red in spots.

"Since when, Josie"?

"Just—just since Sunday."

"I'm certainly sorry to hear that, Josie. What happened?" His voice was the kind that made a person trust him even if they didn't want to. No! She would not tell him. Oh! Never, Never! By the way he looked at her, she could not help but trust him---out it came.

"Miss Simmons said she was ashamed of me!" Josie's lips quivered and big tears welled up in her eyes.

"Oh, no, she told me some very nice things about you, Josie."

"Did she?" The tears splashed on her dress.

"Yes, she did my child. I cannot understand this! There must be some mistake, just tell me all about it."

Brokenly the child told the story. Can a child's heart ache as much as a big one?

"Velda, you know Velda—she never liked me and wouldn't ever sit beside me. She has such pretty dresses and a pretty mother—and she always makes fun of me and laughs at me, and after Sunday School I heard her tell her mother I said such crazy things in class—I was in the corner getting my coat and she didn't see me so I—I— just went over and looked at her—and Miss Simmons came up and Velda's mother told Miss Simmons, I was imprudent and I did not belong in the same class as Velda and I put wrong ideas in all the girl's heads, and who was I anyway?"

The child shook with sobs but did not cry out. Mr. Gowen took her hand in his. Her whole body trembled.

"What did Miss Simmons say Josie?"

"She told Velda's mother she was sorry and ashamed of me and couldn't help it and she dearly loved Velda and maybe I could be promoted. And when—when she—
she noticed me, she said, "Why Josie, I thought you went home. Run along dear or you'll miss your dinner, and she winked at Velda and her mother."

The minister looked into space and knew not what to say. The child shook with sobs. She's ashamed of me! What heartbreaking words! The one she loved and adored had wounded her and it made Velda glad. Mr. Gowen could think of nothing to say to justify Ella Simmons. Could it be her love was changeable as that?

Did he not mention the objective of his visit. How could he? He was stunned. Could it be Ella was that kind of a woman? Could it be she loved the child only for the honor it would bring her? Is that why she wanted him to know she had advanced so in her class. Oh, Ella Simmons!

Still he held the child's hand. Once he brushed something from the corner of his eye. Finally, at last the child sat quiet and was calm.

"Josie," he said at last. You trust me don't you?"

She nodded.

"You can always trust me. May God help me never to hurt your little heart. I must go now. Will you promise me not to feel bad about it any more, and try hard to forget all about it, and read and play and sing and come back next Sunday like always?"

She nodded slightly.

Half an hour later Brother Gowen knocked at the door on another street.

***

"Why, Good evening, Brother Gowen, Come right in."

"Thank you, Ella."

"Take a chair. No, this rocker."

"This one is alright. Thank you. I was up to see Josie Carrington this afternoon."

"Oh were you?" She smiled. Isn't she the most precious child?"

"She is the most remarkable and lovable child, Ella."

"Isn't she though? A little dear. I fell in love with her the first time I met her. I suppose you knew she was one of the children I found in the census?"

"Yes, I thought so."

Silence.

"I suppose you found her ready to join the instruction class?"

"I didn't mention it to her, Ella."

She looked surprised and disappointed.

"I suppose you thought it wasn't best. Of course. I knew you'd know whether to or not, after you talked with her. I'm glad now I never mentioned it to her."

Silence.

It bothered Ella. She could not understand. Brother Growen wasn't himself. She picked another chair and picked at the corner of the table runner.

"I found the child heartbroken over the episode which happened Sunday just after you talked to me."

Ella's face colored and she bit her lips.

"You mean what Velda said? I know it was a shame. Velda is so outspoken and rude sometimes, and Josie is so far advanced that some of the children just can't understand her nor appreciate her. I hated it the worst way. And you know what a jealous disposition Velda's mother has. Really, she gets unreasonable sometimes and says things that I hope she doesn't mean, but I had no idea Josie would be so hurt. She's such a sensitive child."

"I don't think she feels so hurt over what Velda and her mother said. I think she's used to Velda's disposition; but she had implicit confidence in you, Ella. I believe she would have staked her life on your love. She is crushed by what you said."

"Why—why—what did I say?" She was so surprised.

"Did you tell Mrs. Rogers you were ashamed of her and she would probably be promoted?" He looked straight at Ella. Her lips turned white.

"Did you say that? Why, Brother Growen, how could I be ashamed of that precious little child? She knows more that all the other girls put together."

"She said she heard you tell Mrs. Rogers that, and I'm— I'm afraid she may not come back any more."

"Oh, no! If I did say it, I did not mean it. Velda and her mother get me so unstrung."

"Well, Ella, it grieves me that the child is so wounded. We have to be very careful what we say about these little ones God has sent to us. They feel more than we do sometimes." His voice was rich and low.

Silence again.

She looked at the floor. The pattern seemed to move.

"Have you ever read this book, Ella?" He handed her a thin blue book.

"I have read it once years ago, I believe. Her voice was husky and her hand trembled.

"It has helped me so much. I thought I'd pass it on to you. Read it again, Ella. I've read it at least six times and I'm going to read it again soon."

He said, "Good evening," and left. She did not follow him to the door. She sat there, and sat. An hour later she snapped on the light and opened the book, "The Christian's Secret of a Happy Life" by Hannah W. Smith. She read it slowly, carefully, page after page. Consecration, Faith, The

Will, Guidance. Doubts—on she read. Temptation, Failures.' It was morning when she went to bed.

Sunday came, but little Josie was not there. The Minister looked troubled and more so did Ella Simmons. The girls whispered and Velda smiled triumphantly.

The Sunday school was nearly over, when the usher approached Ella with a message. She was wanted at the door. An elderly lady in black met her.

"Are you Miss Simmons?" She asked almost sternly.

"Yes."

"I'm Josie Carrington's grandmother."

Ella caught the post for support, but before she had a chance to say a word the woman went on.

"Josie has a very sore throat and couldn't come this morning; and she wouldn't be quieted until I said I'd bring these library books back, and take two more home for her."

"Why, I'd just be glad to. I'm sorry to hear she's sick. I was going to come to see why she wasn't here. Ella carefully chose two books.

"Thank you for your trouble, Miss Simmons. And here is a note Josie sent along." She handed her a paper tied with a bit of pink string.

"And here is a paper and a card for Josie. Can't you stay for the church services?"

"No thank you. I must get back and take care of Josie."

Ella stepped into the cloakroom and unfolded the note.

"Dear Teacher,

I am sorry I can't come today. My throat is so sore, but if you pray for me, I can come next Sunday. I felt sad and all mixed up inside till I read my second book. It told me how to forgive and forget and be happy again. I love you and won't ever be ashamed of you, I know.

"Josie Dell Carrington."

The children wondered what had become of their teacher. She did not return.

"Mama," lisped little Gladys Smith when they got home from church, "Why, Miss Thimonth was tho nitne to me today. And she let me path the paperth too, and put one word on the blackboard. And we're all going to thee Jothie this afternoon."

In the afternoon Ella Simmons and her class of girls started up the hill toward the Old Lilac Place. The hedge was not blooming, but something was blooming in Ella's heart. For the first time in its history, the walls of the Old Lilac house reverberated with music of children's voices in sacred song. Josie's mother and Father listened, wondering, half afraid. The children prayed and their prayers for Josie's recovery were answered. And for the first time in her life, Ella Simmons spoke to someone about her soul.

Josie came to Sunday school the next Sunday, and three came with her. They kept coming, and in the time of lilacs, some months later, a little child knelt between Father and Mother and was blessed with Holy Baptism, while an elderly woman stood and confessed her sins before God and the people.

A Long Way From Home

By Carol Hostetler Kauffman, age 29, Hesston Kansas
Originally published May 4, 11, and 18, 1931
in the Youth's Christian Companion

Mrs. Tucker watched the car disappear over the hill to the north. Over and over she creased the telegram with the nails of her thumb and second finger, while her mouth hung open in meek surprise. After the car was out of sight she still stared almost as if she expected its driver to come back and get what he had left. At last she read again in six short words she had all but creased in two, slipped the paper into its envelope, and putting it under the edge of a poorly ironed doily on the sideboard, climbed the stairs to the single unfinished room above.

All afternoon the hot sun had been beating down on the little frame house until now the one upper room was like a bake oven. Mrs. Tucker opened the top button of her percale blouse, and pinned up her damp neck ringlets. She lifted the faded and split shades at the two small windows and as she did so the screen-like designs on the floor were replaced by the full rays of the sun.

An old-fashioned iron bed stood in one corner, a trunk in another. Two straight-backed chairs (one broken cane bottom) stood on opposite sides of a bureau which had no mirror. There was no covering on the floor, no curtains at the windows and no scarf on the bureau. One ancient picture of four kittens in a basket hung between two of the studs and an old green umbrella hung from a nail on one of the rafters.

Mrs. Tucker raised the window, and as she did so, a frightened mouse darted out from under the bureau, and disappeared at the opposite side of the room. The woman jumped slightly, then frowned. She frowned more as she brushed her hand over the calico quilt on the bed. It was very dusty. With a swift jerk she pulled it off and shook it vigorously from the window. One corner caught on a rusty clapboard nail, making an ugly snag. Several big flies made their way inside in spite of the waving quilt, and buzzed tormentingly around the room.

Mr. Tucker called, "Is that you up there?"

"Yes."

"Where are you Nance?"

"Why, I'm upstairs here!"

"What you doin up there?"

On the top of the stairs he came to an abrupt stop while an exclamation escaped him. The floor was wet from mopping and the room was straightened up. A clean pillowcase was ready to go on the bed and a clean scarf for the bureau.

"Well," said Mr. Tucker, as he wiped perspiration from his face, "Who are you fixing up for?"

"Who do you think, Chris?"

"You've got me, Nance", he said in blank wonder.

"Well, who did you ask to come and stay sometime?" Her voice had a tone of patience this time.

"Ask? Why, Nance, I've asked the folks to come and see us sometime, didn't you too?"

"But we never expected them to take it seriously enough to stay for the summer."

"Well, he didn't say he'd come for the whole summer."

"Summer!" shouted Mr. Tucker. His eyes almost popped out. They're coming for the whole summer?"

"Well they didn't say they were coming for the whole summer but it sounds as if they are coming maybe for a while anyway."

"Here, Chris, take the broom and pail down for me. I've got to hurry up and bake and gather my senses together. You hurry up and get shaved and get your hair fixed. You're to meet the 10:40 train."

"But I say, Nance," He called back as he hurried to do her commands. "Who all am I to actually meet?"

"The telegram is under the doily on the sideboard. Go and read it."

The man lost no time in finding the right page. With nervous clumsy fingers he pulled it out and read it.

"Milford! Milford! Did I actually ask them to come here?"

"Well, don't you know? You got a letter from him and when you answered, you asked if he couldn't stop and pay us a visit when they come to get some animals."

"So I did, my girl, and he took me up on it! Well, I'm glad he thinks enough of us to stop off."

He returned the telegram under the doily almost tenderly. A lazy smile crept over his face.

"Well, I wouldn't mind if we were having them for company. I'm afraid Milford won't be able to stand it here very long. But we need to get the upstairs room finished to be decent for them.

Chris put a rough hand on his wife's shoulder. "Now Nance." His voice was low and lovingly rich. "Now don't you go a worryin 'bout us not havin things nice enough for Dan's boy. We'll just make the best of what we got. No one can do better than that.

"Now you go ahead and make them pies. I've never tasted any better ones. Please stop worryin.

"I came in to ask you if you would do some fixin on my overalls. I got them caught on the fence out there."

"Well, I guess you did! Come here and I'll sew it up for you right now. Yes, could you bring in the wood? If you stay around here for a while longer you can fix some more things for me. That caster needs to be fixed and the chickens need tending to."

Chris Tucker knew from experience that the easiest and wisest attitude to take was what his good wife showed excitement for, and be extremely calm and patient. It always worked for him. By seven-thirty every chore was done and supper was on the kitchen table by eight.

"Everything's about done now, isn't it? I'll take the rest of those taters if you don't want them.

"I wish I had some curtains for upstairs and something for the floor."

"I thought you already did have curtains at the windows."

"Well Chris, that's just something I had from up in the old trunk. Well, they won't know the difference."

"Is there anything else you need done?"

"Oh, I guess not. Anyway, I'd rather have you help me, than havin half a dozen women. Want to go along to the station? How about goin along to meet the train?"

The train was on time. So were Mr. and Mrs. Tucker. Only two other persons were on the long wooden platform when the train came to a stop. Before it came to a complete stop, a slender black-haired youth caught sight of the two figures beside the mailbox. The youth leaped from the steps and came with outstretched arms, running forward. He lugged a heavy suitcase.

***

"Uncle Chris!" he said most happily, as his outstretched hand caught Uncle Chris' hand and shook it vigorously. Then tenderly he planted a kiss on his shaven cheek. "Aunt Nancy! A kiss for you too.

"It was so great for you to ask me to come! You look just like the pictures I've seen. How are you anyway? It's a shame to make you come after me this time of night, but it's the only connection I could make."

A happy carefree laugh floated through the night. Chris spoke at his first opportunity.

"That's alright, Milford. We're glad to have you come. You're the first of Dan's children to come out this way. Well, they all talked of coming. Chris, that's about as far as they ever come. I'm on my way to Portland and I thought if I'm going this way I'd run down here and spend a week with you."

"To Portland?" demanded Mrs. Tucker, with surprise, and she looked at Chris inquiringly. "That's a long way from home."

"It's a long way from home, but they asked me to come out there and help in their Summer Bible School, and then I'll try to find work and help out in the Mission the rest of the summer. I'm anxious to go."

"You don't say?" Chris Tucker looked up into the face of his brother's boy with a strange mingling of envy and pride. His lower lip quivered. The woman was ready to speak, but the words died on her lips. An indescribable sickness of soul crept over the man also. An old wound had been freshly stabbed. They stood there in the light of the open station door, motionless, speechless, and numb with long-tired hope, and gazed into the face of Milford. Milford—Dan's youngest boy, just Eddie's age, less a month. So tall and straight and open faced. A college freshman and—and a worker in the church—a Bible School teacher. NO! How dare this be—this—unfair lot, this honor to one, this reproach to the other of like flesh and blood!

"Chris, let's go." Mrs. Tucker grabbed her husband's arm fitfully.

"Yes. The car is right over this way, Milford." And as Chris led the way the young man followed, leading Aunt Nancy by the arm.

"I can't tell you how glad I am you came along Aunt Nancy. Mother has talked so often of you to us children. You really don't seem a bit strange to me."

"Don't I?"

"I've often heard about the night you won in the spelling match at Lazy Creek, and about the cherry-tree episode."

"The time I broke my arm?"

"Yes, that's it. And the time you and Uncle Chris had a runaway horse with the cutter, and the time you came to see us when we were little spuds and Eddie and me and Dell all together. A trio of hearty laughter again rang upon the air of the happy memory. It was a beautiful night to be out. The old car sped over the hills without a bit of coaxing. The road ahead of them shone white under the full moon and the air trembled with fragrance from the damp fields.

"Well, this is the place," announced Nance, apologetically as they turned in abruptly to the left. "It's just a humble little place your comin' to Milford but—"

"It's not too humble for me, Aunt Nancy. I've been used to pretty simple life in the dormitory."

"I know we don't have things like you have at home, but we'll give you the—Trix! Get away there. Get away!" Milford bent over and gave the excited animal several friendly pats.

Mrs. Tucker walked ahead and lit a lamp. The house still had the odor of freshly baked bread. Everything was in perfect order and even though it was humble and exceedingly so, it offered to Milford an atmosphere of comfort and home. While Nance prepared her strawberry shortcake to eat, Chris and Milford leaned against the homemade cupboard and talked of pleasant reminiscences. Little did the lad realize how the heart of the jubilant-voiced man burned within him with a penetrating void, more poignant than pain. And with every mouthful of their guest, be he ever so welcome, the woman, whose hair was streaked with gray, could not help wishing another boy were sitting across the table helping to eat the fruit of their garden.

Every time Milford spread his lips in a smile, Nance felt her face contract with shrouded anguish. Every time she allowed her gaze to linger around his eyes while downcast—those lashes—and brows—she had to bite her lip to choke a spasm of agony that pierced her soul. Yet how good he was to look on—not handsome, exactly, but good-looking. There were no visible signs of sin in his life, no deceitful shadows in his eyes, no hypocrisy in his voice.

The clock struck twelve before the three left the table. With a small Kerosene lamp in the hand, held above his head, Mr. Tucker directed Milford to the only guest room they had. The lively air of early morning was making havoc with the curtains and as soon as the lamp was set on the bureau the light went out.

"Well, I guess if you want a light, Milford, we'll have to close one window. There is too much of a draft here. I'll go down and get a match.

"Never mind, Uncle Chris. The moon makes plenty of light tonight and I don't need a lamp to undress anyway. What time do you start doin chores in the morning?"

"Five-thirty. But you sleep till we call you."

"Not for the world, Uncle Chris. If you're going to make me feel like company, I'll leave tomorrow."

"Well, alright then," he chuckled, "I'll see that you get plenty to do."

"That's the system. Now, I can enjoy my bed better."

The man turned abruptly and descended the stairs with a "Good-night!"

"What you thinking about Nance?" Mr. Tucker found his wife sitting on the edge of the bed, her one slipper in her hand, and her eyes fixed rigidly to the opposite wall.

"Oh, Chris," she cried, and her voice broke into a child-like whimper. "Doesn't he—he—remind—you—of—"

"I see it more the longer—I—look Nance." His voice broke into an accompanying whine. Not the whine of whims unhampered, but of disappointment and unjust punishment.

They said very little more lest their voices could be heard in the room overhead, but two tired gray heads tossed restlessly on their pillows until dawn.

"Did you call me, Nance?" It was two thirty and Chris sat up in bed.

"What is it Nance?"

"Nothin' Chris. What's the matter?"

"I thought you called."

"I was only dreaming, I guess."

"Do you feel alright?"

"I think so. Why?"

"You wake me up so often."

"Isn't it time to get up?"

"No, Nance. I wish it was."

The week passed more swiftly than any Nancy Tucker had ever experienced. Every day was a new and pleasant one. She found herself watching the clock eagerly for mealtime to come. She tried recipes she had used when a girl in her mistress's kitchen. Of course, she used half lard when it called for butter and three eggs when it called for four. Nance couldn't use such things at liberty even though she was on a farm. But how Milford did enjoy it all! He lost some of the study-hall complexion and made a few calluses on his hands. As soon as his prayers were offered, the pillow seemed to come up to meet his sleepy head. On the other hand, Nance had a hard time getting to sleep. Always at night her thoughts got the best of her. As for Chris, his daytime spirits were high and the night ones low. Darkness has a way of painting gray things black and sad things sadder—saddest. But the days were unusually pleasant.

***

One evening Milford looked up from a bunch of photographs he had found in the table drawer. Most of them were pictures of days far removed and some were considerably recent. It was on one of these photos that Milford hesitated longest.

He faltered a little, "Have—you—?

"What is it?" asked Chris, and at the same time he caught sight of the picture on top of the pile. He flinched.

"You asked about Eddie?"

"I was going to."

"You heard from him, I suppose?"

"It will be three years." The older man's tone came from his throat like a vibration of a minor string on a wooden instrument. His eyes grew black with fright. His head dropped to his trembling hand. Milford did not venture to make further conversation on the subject. That the subject had been purposely avoided before, was evident, but suddenly he continued on his own accord and his tears came unbidden.

"The last time I heard, he was in Montana working as a rancher. He wrote a letter and said he always got along with her, and now that she's gone—we—never—hear. He wrote just days before, when she was still conscious. She was just conscious enough to know we heard. It seemed she couldn't go until she knew.

A silence fell over the little room. They could hear Nancy crying softly in the kitchen. Milford said not a word. It was not necessary. His silence, his bowed head, and heavy breathing expressed more than any words, however kind. Ten minutes passed. And still not a word. Carefully Milford replaced the pictures, stepped across the room, pressed his rough hand between the two smaller ones and tiptoed upstairs.

Before they knew it, the week had come to an end and the time Milford had for leaving was here. It was almost like giving up again, an only son, to see Milford pack his suitcase and leave. The trip to the depot was a pleasant one, and many were the things of interest of the past week's experiences that were rehearsed by the three. It was all too short a time.

Arrived at the depot, they had but a short time to wait for the westbound train. A strange thrill filled the souls of Uncle Chris and Aunt Nance as the big locomotive rolled in with its inviting train of cars. With a hasty but affectionate goodbye, Milford boarded the train.

Chris and Nance stood on the wooden platform and waved goodbye until the figure at the window was lost in the distance. Wearily, almost reluctantly, they walked back to the car.

"There was so much I was goina' to say when we bid goodbye, but I somehow forgot it all when the time came." Nance gave a peculiar sigh.

"I was goina say some things too an' I said somethin' altogether different. I wonder if he really enjoyed himself as he seemed to. Wonder if he actually wanted to work so hard. He nearly spoiled me."

"I hope we made him feel repaid for stoppin."

"Nance, why did you seem so kinda upset about it the day you got the telegram?"

"Well, Chris, I'll jes tell you. Not knowin' what he'd be like, I was jes afraid maybe he'd ask a lot of questions 'bout Eddie and rub it in or try to show off. I was jes afraid it would get the best of me."

"You—you never were sweeter, Nance."

They drove home in silence, but those words of Chris fell like dew on her thirsty heart. All the way home and for weeks afterward, it strengthened and refreshed her.

The summer slipped by. Most of the canning was over, and Chris was cutting corn. It had been what farmers call a prosperous year.

Chris was cutting corn close to the road when the mail carrier drove up, so Chris came out for the mail. He was expecting a check from the creamery. It came. Another letter also—he caught his breath and ran toward the house.

Nance saw him coming and ran white-faced to meet him.

"What's the matter, Chris?" She cried.

"Sit down here beside me, Nance." Instantly she recognized the handwriting. Together as one mind, one tense soul, they read.

"What's the matter, Chris?" she cried again.

Portland, Oregon
Sept 9

Dear Mother and Father,

It is six years since I left you in a fit of anger, but I've never been able to blot you out of my mind. You come before me in every bad place I've even been, and Dell's face follows me day and night. I've tried everything to be able to forget. Several weeks ago I stumbled into a little mission in town. I don't know why I did it, but I heard singing and went in. I heard a young fellow talk that night and it seemed he was talking straight to me. I'll never forget as long as I live what he said. I couldn't forget it. He haunted me all night. On another night I heard him in a street meeting. His words branded my soul. If I knew his name I'd try to find him tonight, but I'm in

*the hospital now with blood poisoning in my left hand. The
doctor says I may lose it.*

*Oh, I've lots of tough days, mother and father, and it's
been nothing but knocks and trouble; but I'm coming home as
soon as I'm able. I'm coming back to start over if you'll take
me.*

*God has forgiven me. Will you? Oh, Dad, will you trust
me again? I'm coming home to do the things I refused to do,
and I'm going to put a mirror in the bureau for the one I
smashed that night I left. My arm pains me terribly. I never
realized before, I was such a long way from home. God bless
you till I come.*

Your Wayward Boy,
Eddie

Chris Tucker clasped the wet tear-stained letter tight to
his dusty jacket and lifted his face to heaven; while Nance
bowed hers toward the steps.

DALE'S DIARY

By Christmas Carol Kauffman, age 29, Hesston, Kansas
Originally published June 7, 1931
in the Youth's Christian Companion

June 8

Vacation at last! Ma let Martha and I sleep till 8:30 this morning just to see how it would seem not to have that alarm ring. I didn't sleep much after seven anyway, but I acted sleepy when Ma called. Ma had the wash ready for Martha to hang out and the line broke just when she got it about full. Such a time! I found a piece of wire in the wood shed and pieced it out where it had rusted and Ma and Martha both got kinda excited. I sure like Monday dinners---chicken, gravy and Sunday leftovers, and strawberries I gathered. It seems like those that ripen over Sunday always taste the best. I figured all afternoon. I sold 35 birdhouses and made $39.50 above expenses. I invested $5.00 of that in aster plants and gladiola bulbs. They look fine. I decided today to invest the rest in a refreshment stand out front. Pa gave his permission. I'm going to select my lumber tomorrow.

June 9

I started my stand today. Pa sure acts like a boy. I wonder what kind of a boy he was? I spent $3.00 for second hand lumber and the rest will go for lemons and sugar and ice for lemonade, popcorn and butter and snacks. That's all I'm going to handle. Ma said she can show us how to make the best lemonade and popcorn in town. Since we're on the highway, I know it will sell. Martha is going to invest her quarter in it too, and buy lemons over and over with her profits. It's getting hotter every day too, which will help my trade. Everybody in the neighborhood wanders what I am makin. I tell you, it pays to keep still and mind your own business in business. I think it pays to be confidential with God about it though. He sure blessed me with my birdhouses. Amen!

June 10

I like dogs, but when one man keeps four bulldogs, there's something wrong. Stoners dogs took Mary Jane down today and would have tore her to pieces if I wouldn't have rescued her and stoned them away. Her mother gave me a piece of fresh pumpkin pie for it too. I see in tonight's paper that the City Health Department will pay 25 cents for every pound of trapped flies. Pa said he'd help me fix a trap of screen. Martha said girls can't ever earn anything and Ma said Pa should help fix two traps and quick as a wink, Ma selected the smelliest place for Martha's trap. I didn't say anything, thinking of that preference' lesson we had in Junior Meeting and I was one of the speakers.

June 11

I get so interested in this stand I hate to stop and peddle papers, but Ma says it's the wonderfullest blessing to have lots to do. We're going to start business tomorrow. I'm glad Martha is in this too, cause she'll wash the tumblers for me and take charge while I peddle papers. Ma wrote the dandiest sign I'll paint on each side and front:

ICE COLD LEMONADE
GOOD AND SWEET
BUTTERY POPCORN
BEST YOU'LL MEET

I wonder if I'll sleep tonight?

June 12

We had Prayer Meeting tonight instead of last night because so many people wanted to go to Clifton to hear some Dr. from China give a lecture. We didn't go, but since Pa has been so nice to me, I didn't beg. If our tires were better we would have. I wish I would find some treasure box somewhere and I'd buy a couple new tires and surprise him. I don't know why people don't write true to life stories. I never found a treasure box yet or shot a lion or found strawberries as big as apples. I told Mr. Berman about my new plan to raise missionary money. He looked surprised, then slapped my back. I didn't get quite ready today. Ma said Saturday is the best day to open anyway.

June 13

"A poor beginning and a good ending" they say. If this is a poor beginning, what will the end be? I sold 23 glasses of lemonade and 17 sacks of popcorn. Just enough popcorn left for us to eat tomorrow. If I only didn't have to collect on Saturday, Ma says Martha can't help her much sitting out there all afternoon, but Ma didn't say it a bit cross like. Here's a great poem I found.

LET US BE BETTER MEN

Let us be better men;
Let us find things to do
Saner and sweeter than any yet,
Higher and nobler and true!

Let us be better men!
Let us begin again,
Trying all over the best we know
To climb and develop and grow.
Let us be better men!
Whether we pick or pen.
The labor we do is a work worth while
If our hearts are clean and our spirits
smile.
And out of the rick and rust and stain
We made some growth and we mark
some gain.
Let us be better men!
In a world that needs so much
The loftier spirit's touch.
Let us grow towards the light,
Wedded to wanting to do the right
Rather than wedded to human might.

—Wellspring.

June 14

Say, but the cars go fast on Sunday. And they all look at my
stand and some slow down, then go on so disappointed like. I
wonder why it would be so awful wrong to make some missionary money on Sunday? Pa explained it all to me today, but
why do the wicked prosper? How come others can and we
can't? I've got a bunch of questions to ask Mr. Berman sometime. There's a heap of other things I wonder about too.

June 15

It rained all day and part of the time it poured. I had to close
my stand. I sold two glasses of lemonade, one to the bread
man and one to the mailman. We didn't make much so there

wasn't much loss. If I sell once, I'll sell again, meaning—Ma knows how all right. Some of the youngsters want to trade for pins. I said, "Nothin stirring, I'm not going to start a notion counter."

June 16

This was a grand day for business. Martha's quarter has made her 90 cents already. The grocer across the street is glad we get our lemons and butter there and he made us a special price on sacks. Seems like God is on our side. The missionary Dr. is coming to our church tomorrow night. I'm glad now I didn't beg to go to Clinton. I'm going to sit on one of the front seats. I hope he has things to show and talks in Chinese.

June 17

I'd sure like to go to China. He had me up in front and help him hold things. I wish I was 21 right now. Mr. Berman called a class meeting tomorrow night right after Prayer Meeting. I wonder what he's got for us now? Since our other contest closed and Tim got the Bible and I got the Testament, we haven't been doing anything special.

June 18

What will I do now? The Summer Bible School opens on Monday and will last for 2 weeks. I can't ask Ma to keep my stand. That's what Mr. Berman talked about mostly, and a way to earn a pocket knife with our own name on one side and a Scripture verse on the other: to get one child and one grownup to come to Sunday School, and they become a regular member. The child won't be so hard but how about the grownup? That's hard. Nobody acted very rapturous about it, but the knife he said, that's just our earthly prize, but I'd sure like to have one. Who will keep my stand from 9:00 to 12:00 every morning? Who could I trust?

June 19

The question is still unsolved!????

June 20

Martha had a pound of flies this morning and I half a pound. Where do they all come from? There must be millions and billions of them in our neighborhood. I wish I could talk to Solomon and he could tell me who to get. I got the best letter today from South America. John and I are going to keep on even if our contest is closed.

June 21

George had a dirty little fellow to Sunday School today. He said he lives in an old freight car out by the water tower. He never saw a Sunday School before and he sure acted dazed. I must find someone before next Sunday. It's easy to get them to come once, but it isn't so easy to get them to keep on coming. I tried it already and it depends upon the teacher we have, I believe. We went to Lakes for dinner today. The girls did the dishes and Martha broke one of Mrs. Lake's best tumblers and cried until Mrs. Lake said she didn't care one bit. Martha says she knows she did care. I wish girls wouldn't cry so easy. Mr. Lake told how a man came there with ferrets and they killed 73 rats for him. Beings they don't have any boys, I stayed in and listened to the men talk. I got an idea.

June 22

I went over to Dellmar's early and got Jeff to keep my stand. He's got only one leg and a crippled hand. I don't know him much except I heard Mr. Lake tell, but I'm going to trust him and give him half of what he sells. That's good pay and he made 60 cents this morning. It was good and hot today. Business was rushing this afternoon but not so rushing that I can't study my lessons in between. It's mostly rushing for Martha. She gets tired popping all the corn. I suppose I will have to take pity and trade places more. There were 80 at Bible School today. Miss Crane can't lead singing very good.

June 23

I forgot to write. I was figuring all morning.

June 24

I had a flat on my bike tonight. I never got home till after seven. Ma sure was worried and we had company besides. He's a school chum of Pa's. I have to sleep on the davenport tonight. I hope he stays a while. I could listen to him talk all evening. He used to be a cowboy.

June 25

Jeff Delmar went along with me to Prayer Meeting tonight, and I never had to ask him twice. He's my prospect for a grown-up. I thought of it all at once. There is something awful strange about him. I don't know what, but I like him.

THE 'FINING POT

By Christmas Carol Kauffman, age 29, Halstead, Kansas
Originally Published September 13, 20, and 27, 1931
in the Youth's Christian Companion

1219 Woodring Blvd.
Beldon, Wisconsin
June 25, 1931

Dear Mother,

I'm exasperated almost beyond words. Don't tell me I'm excited over nothing. It's no small thing. Mrs. Dantoe is simply furious with me again this morning because I didn't have the napkins placed just so to suit her, and they had only soup for dinner last night, And some Mr. Denison came from New York. He wore a red tie and a gold stick pin and he used his dinner fork for his salad too, and took his fingers to eat his cheese, but I don't suppose she even noticed that. Oh Mother, she is so impossible. I don't think there is another girl in Beldon who has to work for a crazy woman like mine. Sometimes I wish I had come home for the summer and gone back to Clawson's even if I do get more here. I think my nerves will snap. If Mr. Dantoe and Carolyn were not as nice to me as you are, I would leave today. Carolyn is really sweet to me, even though she is a rich society girl. I know she goes to a lot of places just to satisfy her mother. They have regular squabbles sometimes because Carolyn would rather sit at home and read. And every time she gets alone by herself when her mother is away, she comes into the kitchen and talks with me. If her mother knew it, I suppose I would get fired on the spot. And when the rest of the family was gone, Mr. Dantoe would come into the kitchen to wipe the dishes for me too. Dear me! What would her ladyship say? Every chance he gets, he asks me

89

about our beliefs, and why and etc. He isn't just inquisitive. I could tell. Whenever she leaves----she wanted me to hold her dress as she got in the car. She often takes her dog. She will not be here for dinner. What a relief! And this is my afternoon off. I think I will go over to Granny Hanes. She can always cheer me up so.

Bless her heart, every time I go there she feels like she has to give me something. Last time she gave me an old fashioned cream pitcher. Just a tiny thing, but I love it anyway. You remember I told you she gave me a wooden tray. I dropped it yesterday and broke the handle off. Too bad.

Dad said your garden looks so nice. It rained here for over two weeks. But you'd never know it by the looks of the lawns. The sprayer is on from morning till night and they have all kinds of choicest vegetables and fruits. I wish I could send home what they throw away. I hate to do it, but she won't eat leftovers (if she knows it) Sometimes I fix them up and she thinks it's something new and wonderful. Really, she has given me a few compliments.

Mother, what shall I do about my white dress? I washed it carefully by hand, but it has shrunk all out of reason. Shall I send it home for Mabel? I wish I had one-fifth of the shoes and dresses Gwendolyn doesn't wear anyway.

I wish you'd tell me what to do, Mother. Shall I stay here and be talked to like I was some old slave, or shall I try to find another place? I didn't tell what she said. I don't want to, but sometime, I'm afraid I'll just explode to her face. This is ruining my disposition and making my whole summer drudgery. Don't you pity me at all? You've never said much, but I guess you can't realize.

Lots of love,
Goldie

***

Temple, Ohio
June 21, 1931

My Dear Goldie,

It is nine thirty. I suppose you are busy with your work yet. I should think it would be lovely to handle all those beautiful dishes and silverware. I always had an eye for pretty dishes. You can be glad you don't have to launder all those linen tablecloths, napkins and towels. Don't you remember how you worked at Simsons?"

I canned thirty-five quarts of cherries yesterday. They looked so nice, but many of them were wormy. But I am thankful for what I have. Lots of people have nothing to can and there are lots of Temple girls, still hunting for work. Be strong and of good courage, Goldie. Ralph got a two-dollar cut in his wages Saturday, but he was not the only one.

We were invited to John's for dinner Sunday. Everything was simple, but so good. Poor Rachel gets those pains in her side again and John is rather worried she will have to have an operation. Little Rosalie is such a sweet child. She doesn't act like most children, but sits around so quiet as though she were thinking.

You said in your last letter you couldn't sleep at night. Now Goldie, you must just dismiss the things of the day and relax. I am sending you this little poem to hang beside your bed. Read it over before you go to bed and I'm sure it will help you.

Many of the girls, and other folks too, ask about you. Mrs. White takes such an interest in you. Of course, I always tell them you are getting along all right, but have a hard place. After Mrs. Dantoe knows you better, and you know her, it will go better. So often when the lady is so nice at first, it turns out the other way. Just do your best, Goldie, and be willing to learn all you can. It will never come amiss. I think of you most of the time and wonder what you are dong and wish I could have had your experience when I was a girl. We are all busy but well. I want to make James a suit this afternoon.

Good-bye, Much love,
Mother

P.S. James said, "Hello to Goldie."

***

Temple, Ohio
June 28, 1931

Dearest Girl, Goldie,

I trust by this time the little poem I sent you has helped you. We must learn to live above the disagreeable things in life. Not that I think you felt bad over nothing, Goldie, but the world is hunting for girls who can take knocks and abuse and be all the sweeter be-cause if it. Do I pity you, dear child? Of course I do, but I might sit down and cry for you a whole day and it wouldn't help matters one bit. I doubt if it would ever help if you could cry. I imagine she is the kind of woman who resents such an attitude. Why not turn around and pity her?

Anyone can fly into a rage or talk cross without half trying, but it takes strength of character and real womanhood to keep back the words that want to come out. Don't do it, Goldie. You would feel only worse afterwards. How often we say things which later we would like to take back. Perhaps Mrs. Dantoe was a spoiled child. Maybe she was never taught differently. You were, Goldie. And maybe she is testing you to see what you are made of. They know what you profess. If it does not make you different from her, what more have you?

Dear girl, I know I have not said much, but do not think I have passed it over lightly. It has been a burden on my heart and I pray daily, not only that your lady will be more reasonable, but also that you will have the grace to take it. If you suffer for doing wrong what is that? But if you suffer even though you are right, and take it patiently, that is pleasing to God. Read I Peter 2:20. (For what glory is it, if , when ye be buffeted for your faults, ye shall take it patiently? but if, when ye do well, and suffer for it, ye take it patiently, this is acceptable with God,) I must read it often too. You know all the things Amy Croup has said about us. Poor ignorant woman! She will have to give an account of all of it herself.

Dear, it is too bad about your white dress. If you want to send it home for Mabel, I will send you material for a new one. You need a better one for the chorus next fall anyway. How glad I am you are handy with the needle.

No, I would not be in a hurry to look for another place, Goldie. Maybe it would turn out to be worse. You can at least be glad Gwendolyn and Mr. Dantoe are nice to you and I think it is very kind of him to come for you after church. Be wise, Goldie. Remember who you are, and what you represent, and answer Mr. Dantoe's questions according to scripture. I think you know without my mentioning it, that you must never allow him to show any personal interest in you, nor you with him.

With a mother's concern,

Mother

***

1219 Woodring Road
Beldon, Wisconsin
July 1, 1931

Dearest Mother,

I cleaned silverware this morning until I was almost blue in the face. We are beginning to get ready for Saturday night.

There will be fifty guests in honor of Gwendolyn's 17th birthday. Of course they will dance. I suppose it will be morning before I get out of the kitchen. She is getting a caterer and three girls to help serve, but you can't conceive of the work it all takes, and Mrs. Dantoe gets so excited. She calls up the Bakery and Ice Cream Co. every day to remind them about the frozen figures that are to be here at such and such an hour and not a minute after. Oh yes, she has ordered ice cream in the figures of 17 and decorated with real read rosebuds.

I'll confess, I haven't exploded to Mrs. Dantoe's face yet, but I came very close to it several times. She is actually rude even to her husband. I don't believe she loves him a bit. All she thinks about is herself and her fancy society clothes. The poem has helped a little Mother. It is so idealistic. I thought though that not very many in my place could live up to it.

Oh, you need never fear, there will never be a personal interest between Mr. Dantoe and myself. He is very respectful of me and almost fatherly to me. He is so homely and has an ugly nose, but still there is something appealing about him. How two different personalities even attract each other is more than I can see.

Between you and me, Mrs. Dantoe is beautiful and looks adorable in black with her golden hair and blue eyes, and if you turn around and take a second look, Gwendolyn is still prettier, even though she almost has her father's nose. I wish I had hair like hers.

By the way, Mother, I must tell you one thing. The other day, Mrs. Dantoe was coming down the stairs all dolled up in her blue chiffon dress. She was going to a bridge party and she was nervous all morning because her hat hadn't come yet. She had it made to match her dress. In some way she caught one of her dress ruffles on the key of her desk, and when she got up it ripped it off about nine inches. I never heard a woman use such horrible words. I ran over and said, "What a shame, but that can easily be fixed."

"Fixed," she screamed. "Who in the world can fix this now? It is time to go!"

"I can fix it." I said. And off she tore her dress and she had it on again in ten minutes. I don't believe anyone ever noticed it. I know it pleased her so, that I could fix it for her. She's been a little kinder to me ever since. And, yesterday she asked me to sew some lace on a dress for Gwendolyn and also some buttons on her sport jacket, and thanked me profusely.

But, oh dear, this morning she was on her regular rampage again, not only at me, but with everyone. I am getting over the idea of ever having an outburst with her. In fact, I'd almost be afraid to try it; for I am not used to it. There are times when I actually tremble, when I hear her coming, yet I never heard anyone talk so sweet over the phone. I think she might have many friends, because sometimes she spends most of the forenoon at the phone.

I can't say I exactly pity Mrs. D, but I do pity Gwendolyn. She seems unhappy much of the time, and once she told me she wished she could take up nurse's training or something worth while, but her mother wouldn't agree to it. She said she wished she could get her hands all mess up in berries or something to see how it felt. Oh, my no, she must be a lady! But, one morning when her mother was shopping she just begged me till I let her mix and roll some pie dough. She didn't know any more how to than a child. Her mother said the pie was very good and Gwendolyn gave me a wink to keep mum about it. No, I'll never tell.

I will send the white dress home for Mabel. That is nice of you Mother, to send me new material. Say "Hello" to all the girls. Tell Edna I will write some day. Don't work too hard, Mother.

Love,
Goldie

***

Temple, Ohio
July 7, 1931

My dearest Goldie,

I was wondering how your day was on the 4th. Father's and my Sunday School classes and their families went out to Creek Falls. We had a lovely time, but oh, it was so hot. I never saw Mrs. Mayer enjoy herself so much since Perry died. It did us all good to hear her laugh again. The children all waded in the water and we all sat on the bank. Joe Troup gave such a good talk on "Christ, a Social Leader."

I mailed the material for your dress yesterday. I enclosed a few patterns and material for a school dress.

Did you hear from the business manager yet? I would rather see you get the sweeping since you have done dishes all summer.

Well, Cordelia and Ed were married on Saturday afternoon at her brother's home and Rev. Grove preformed the ceremony. They have a little place rented on the edge of town close to the reservoir, and she will keep on working. Folks tried to have them married for years, but I thought that was their personal affair. They look as happy as two larks. I believe she has a good husband.

Goldie, do you have time or take time to keep up your devotions? I am wondering if you will finally hanker for that kind of living too. The things that shock us at first become to be a matter of course; then before we realize it, we uphold them. You need your devotions much more now then when you were in school. I was in favor of your going there, and yet I realized how bewitching, how fascinating such a life appeals to a girl of your type. I hope Gwendolyn never gives you any of her cast off clothes. How strange you would look, Goldie. Many a girl has lost spiritually with such a beginning. I know it has been rather hard for you to take advice of this kind, but, dear, I mean it lovingly and because I would have you go back to school stronger because of your summer's experience. Write and tell me more about yourself. It is you I am interested in.

Tenderly,
Mother

***

Beldon, Wis.
July 19, 1931

Dearest Mother,

I haven't heard from you since the 9th of July. I hope nothing is the matter. Lots of things have been the matter here. You know I told you Mrs. D. was nicer after I did that little sewing for her. Well, that lasted several days. Then Tuesday afternoon while she was entertaining, an ugly black cat came walking in. I never saw the cat before, and I don't know yet how it got in, but she blamed me for being careless about the doors, and even accused me of petting and feeding it on the sleight, and of course, I denied it all, but she wouldn't believe me. Oh, Mother, she talked terrible to me and if ever I hated anyone I did her then. I made up my mind I'd taken enough. After supper I went up to my room and packed my suitcase and after dark I slipped down the back stairs and went over to Granny Banes. She was just getting ready for bed, but she took me right in.

Oh, Mother, I wish you knew Granny Banes. She is sure one old dear. I don't know how she ever did it but she talked and talked and got me down beside her bed and prayed with me till she had me promise I'd go back. She said it was all good for me and making me stronger and said a lot of things I couldn't understand. The things she said sounded so wild and unjust, yet I could tell she loved me. I can't tell why I did it, but I promised I'd go back and stayed with Granny all night and slipped up to my room early the next morning. Somehow the hate was all gone. I got up and prepared breakfast as usual and you should have seen them stare at me. About midnight Mrs. Dantoe's brother from St Paul came and, of course, Mrs. D. wanted to have a lunch for him, and came up to my room after me. I left a note on my dresser saying they should mail my check to Mrs. Banes. Gwendolyn told me the next day her mother wanted to come right after me, but she didn't want her brother to find out what happened so she told him the girl was away for the night, so she got out something to eat. Fortunately for her, there were several dainty leftovers in the refrigerator. I've never found out what she intended to eat for breakfast, but she came into the kitchen and threw her arms around me and called me, dear, and said how glad she was that I came back, and she's never accuse me of letting a cat in again, and that she never had a girl she liked as well as me or kept this long, and said she was going to give me a $2.00 raise.

It was too much for me. I couldn't grasp it all just then. I can't really comprehend it yet. Mr. Dantoe also came out and talked to me and apologized for his wife's conduct, and said how he appreciated a Christian girl, one could trust and depend upon in the home, and he said the grocery bill has been from five to ten dollars less a month than when they had any other girl. I'm glad I came back, just for his sake. I know she must talk awful to him sometimes, and I pity him.

Well, Mother, I had been rather neglecting my devotions until after this. Somehow it's different now. I think it took Granny Barnes to get me started. But before I was so wrought up I couldn't calm down much of the time. But now, I don't believe it would make any difference what she'd say to me. Something has made me love her. I'd do anything to please her. It all happened over there at Granny Banes. I can even sing while I work now. I've already promised I'd come back next summer if I can.

No, dear Mother, I do not hanker after this life. Maybe I did a little before, but now I pity them. They are slaves to society and Mrs. Dantoe is so nervous all the time. Some day I expect to see her have a nervous collapse. Granny Barnes said this was my "fining pot." Maybe so, but I am not "fined" to silver yet. This summer is half gone. Mother, write to me.

Love,
Goldie

I KNOW

By Christmas Carol Kauffman, age 28, Halstead, Kansas
Originally published September 27, October 3, 10 & 18, 1931
in the Youth's Christian Companion

The Strievelys were a self-respecting, honest, hard-working family who kept a boarding house in a small town in western Kansas. They were peaceable, temperate, unsophisticated and God-fearing people. The neighbors and patrons were not long in discovering these facts.

Mr. Strievely, who kept a fruit-stand in connection with the boarding house, was a man of marked friendly and likable disposition, but a man not to be trifled with, especially in business transactions. If his first answer to a question was "No" he meant "No" and not maybe. Every salesman had learned this, too.

Mrs. Strievely was a woman of small stature, but fleshy, who spoke as one fairly well educated. She was very industrious. Together they made a good team for the accomplishment of any task, great or small—yes, except one. They wondered at that. They wondered much and still knew little more.

It had to do with Kate. Kate, that tall blithe, fair-faced daughter of eighteen. The other two children displayed the family characteristics without any extreme. But Kate! Mr. and Mrs. Strievely, with their wisdom and authoritative ability combined, failed to cope with the problem she presented.

"Well, but Mother," persisted Kate (in a tone of voice she would not be using were an admirer of hers within hearing), "I don't see how you can figure out that' that makes a particle of difference." She fastened her belt and walked to the mirror. "I'm not Althea Ward and I wouldn't want to be. We aren't alike in anything. We're the opposite. So why do I have to act and dress and live like she does? Althea isn't perfect." She gave her nose a pat with her puff.

"I know she isn't perfect, Kate, I only said she wasn't going."

"Well, maybe she doesn't want to go; maybe she wasn't asked to go." This last was said with glad exultation and a grin of jealous defeat accompanied her nod.

"Clifford Marrow asked her," the mother said softly.

"He never!" Kate's hands fell to her sides like lead. "How do you know?"

"Her mother was here today."

"And what else did she have to say? Kate held her head high and lifted her eyebrows.

"She said Althea wanted to go and told him she would, then after she thought it over she called him up and said she couldn't."

"Couldn't I suppose her mother decided it for her and told her she couldn't. I'd hate to tell a beau of mine I **couldn't** go to such and such a place because my mamma said I couldn't." Kate turned to the mirror and started combing her hair jerkily.

"Mrs. Ward said she left it all up to Althea and she didn't know she told him she couldn't go this morning."

"Well, Why can't she go? She's been wanting a date with Cliff for months, maybe years, for all I know, and now when he finally did ask her—" The sentence was finished with a sneer sent through her nose.

"She said she didn't think it was the place for a Christian and she couldn't feel right in going even if there were a lot of others there."

"Well, there're are sure going to be a lot of people there, all right, I know."

"I suppose so." Admitted Mrs. Strievely, feebly. She stroked her forehead.

Someone knocked. The mother turned toward the door and spoke over her shoulder.

"I wish you'd think it over again, Kate. Someday you may wish you hadn't gone."

"No, I won't; I **know** I won't; and I **know** it's alright to go."

The next evening just before dark Mrs. Strievely and Martin Brobaugh, Marty, (what everyone called him) started off with a few other couples to the caverns. What a wonderful ride! Oh, what an experience, accompanied with many laughters. The dazzling, ever-changing, never ending mixture of color. Bright lights, soft lights, big lights, tiny lights, red lights, blue lights, green lights! Music! Red music, blue music, purple music and screaming orange music, band music, music everywhere. The merry-go-round, the chance booths, the topsy-turvy and the Ferris Wheels. Those pretty girls, so graceful and dancing to the music; so graceful. Of course they did not go inside the bars but they watched, watched and **watched** with quickening and widened eyes, saying nothing, buried in the on-lookers.

At last they must move on, but their thoughts followed them, even after they were gone and on the highway. The music in the wheels of the car and this music memory in their brains, and swaying, gliding memory of those gay couples, head on shoulder brought a kiss on the cheek. They ate on the way home, whether it be popcorn or crackerjack or candy; whatever it was, it mattered not. They talked little.

"You sure missed a well time last night," Kate said to Althea over the phone. "It was a grand night to be out."

"I know it was, Kate."

"I was surprised you turned him down."

"Oh, that." she giggled. "I didn't turn him down. I only turned down the place. We went to the Lutheran church to hear the gospel Quartette."

"You did?" Pause—cough. I don't know anything about it. I—I don't know anything about it."

"Oh yes, they were wonderful musicians—so impressive. They sang for an hour and a half, and all their selections were sacred. 'Like as a Father' I'll never forget its beauty. It was so sweet and tender."

"Was there a big crowd?"

"The church was full. There were only a few of our people there, too."

"Was there a big crowd at the Caverns?"

"Oh, I should say."

"Well I told Cliff I just couldn't justify going there. And he told me after the end of church, he was glad we didn't go to the Caverns. He said he's been there three times and always comes home disappointed."

"Well! Well, I want to wash my dress tonight yet, so I guess I'd better get going."

"Are you coming to the Bible Study class tonight?"

"Oh, I hardly think so. I'd like to, but I'm so tired and I don't have my lesson prepared yet."

"I'm rather tired, too, but it always blesses me to go. And I can get my lesson done some other time."

"Well, that's nice, but it wouldn't matter either way with me. I simply wouldn't."

***

Kate washed and pressed her dress and after eating a few bites of supper and helping with the dishes, she flopped into a chair in the library with her French. Two hours later she went to bed with her lesson only half done, but she wasn't sleepy.

"Kate," called Mr. Strievely from the fruit stand the next evening. "Would you come here a minute, please? Give Mrs. Tayler a dozen oranges while I wait on these customers."

"Rushing business this evening?" Beamed Mrs Tayler from under her sun umbrella.

"Looks like it, doesn't it," Returned Kate with a smile.

"My, how you're growing, Kate. Seams like yesterday you were playing around here on that little red tricycle."

Kate laughed and blushed, for Cliff Marrow was standing near and heard. Why should she care if he heard? Strange, but she did.

"And now you're a young lady," continued Mrs. Tayler as she reached into her bag for the change, "And the pride and concern of your father's heart. I know." she added, as she reached for the sack, "because Millie was your age once, too, and pretty and smart, and Pa would have done anything to help her, but she *knew it* all. She didn't need any advice till it was too late. Not saying you're that sort, Kate! I'm sure you're not, only you put me in mind of her a lot of late. You never knew Millie; she's been dead these twelve years now."

"Poor Millie", whispered Mrs. Tayler, and trotted away.

"What will you have Cliff?" Kate forced a smile as she addressed him.

"Mother sent me after a bushel of peaches. One and a quarter? I guess you'll take my check? Never mind, Mr. Strievely, I'll carry them to the car."

"Cliff's a pretty nice chap, isn't he?" Spoke Mr. Strievely to Kate after the customers had all left.

"What makes you think so?" Kate's lower lip got long and she fumbled with the lemons.

"What makes you think he isn't?" Inquired her father abruptly.

"I didn't say he wasn't."

"But you rather infer it in your answer. As far as I can see he's a nice boy."

"Well, that depends on what you call nice. He *thinks* he's nice. That's what you call big-headed and self-righteous."

"I'm surprised to hear it, Kate. I never noticed it, but I guess you know him better than I do."

"I sure do, and I *know* he's proud and selfish. I don't call that nice."

She turned on her heels and started out of the house.

"Just a minute, Kate," called her father gently. "I want to talk to you a little. You asked your mother this morning for five dollars. Why don't you come to me for the money when you need it?

Kate did not answer, but tightened her lips.

"I have never refused you anything when you needed it, have I?"

A soft, "No."

"What is it that you need now?" He spoke very tenderly to her.

No answer.

"You don't care to tell me, Kate?"

Still no answer. Two little red spots appeared on her face.

"It is for—"

"No, it's not for slippers." Kate could see her father's eyes look to the floor, then she moved her pretty feet as if to hide them.

"That isn't what I was going to ask for. I wanted to know if it's for something you need or something you think you need because you want it."

"Well," she snapped with a toss of her head, while a big tear stood in each eye.

"I never have asked for money for frivolous things, and if you can't trust me to spend it for something I really need, you can keep it. I'll go threadbare before I ask for another dime!"

"Kate." Her father's voice was hurt and broken. He stepped forward, but she backed up indignantly. "Kate, what am I keeping this stand and boarding house for, but to support my wife and children. It is my greatest pleasure to get the things you need and want. I—"

"I don't believe it!" She caught herself. "I—I mean," she added in a softer voice. (After all she had a certain fear of her father. It was only of late that she even dared talk to him like this. She was almost furious at herself,)

"You don't ever think I need anything, and you think I'm arrogant and spend too much, and always want more than other girls." She caught his disappointing glance. "Yes, you do. I know you do!" and sobbing she ran to the house. Just then Marty passed and honked and she didn't wave; then immediately repented of it and wondered what he'd think. Some fathers would have slipped some dollar bills into Kate's room to be found the next morning, but Mr. Strievely was not some fathers, nor most fathers. If Kate couldn't say, couldn't decide to say for what she wanted, then he couldn't see fit to give it to her.

Two weeks later Kate still dreamed that she owned a certain little jacket from Clyde Mail Order Company, but she was too proud to confess she needed it. It was getting colder and she did need it. And she would look appealingly sweet in it. Blanche had mentioned that she just knew she didn't have to beg her father for money.

"Father," Said Mrs. Strievely one evening after they had gone to their room. "What are you going to do about Kate?" Mr. Strievely dropped on the edge of the bed. And rested his head in his hands. It seemed to weigh a lot on him.

"What now?"

"She's getting more stubborn and selfish every day. I can hardly tell her anything and I am shocked at the way she talks back to us. It's an awful example to the other children. Somewhere, sometime we must use the rod or give in, or somehow we can't use our authority now. When Kate was little I never imagined she'd become a problem at eighteen. Oh dear—It pains me the way she runs around with Marty-what's-his-name. I wouldn't say a word if they'd go to places we'd approve of. Now, Saturday night they're going over to Loveland, and you know what that is like."

"She's not going." Mr. Strievely unlaced his shoe with fingers of spunk.

"Well, Father, I'm going to leave it all up to you."

"Did you talk to her about it?"

"Yes. But Ina and Francine are going, so what can I say?"

"Why don't you mothers get together and set your foot down on this?"

"Why don't you talk to Mr. Brubaugh? Why does he allow Marty to run around the way he does?"

"Allow him? Yes, why do we allow our children to do the things they do? When we were young we said how we'd lay down the law and ours would do so and so. Look how we criticized people who couldn't control their children and now we aren't doing any better ourselves. It's easier to say how to do a thing than to do it. "But," Asserted Mr. Strievely emphatically, Saturday night Kate is not going to Loveland."

Mrs. Strievely made no comment but put forth several heavy sighs as she knelt beside the bed.

* * *

Thursday slipped by and Mr. Strievely was busy and failed to have a chance to talk to Kate alone. Friday passed and he was even busier or else she was. At least they never happened to face each other all alone all day. Mr. Strievely decided to talk to Kate before she went to bed, then a chum called and accepted Kate's invitation to stay over the night and they made real a slumber party out of it. From below it sounded more like a "Talk and Laugh Party," than a slumber party. Saturday came and the girl was still there for dinner and the two were having "a lark" making candy, I suppose for the evening.

"It would be a shame," thought the father to himself, "to tell you her now. I should have done it on Wednesday already, but she's **not** going. For once, I'm going to say "NO" to this. That's settled."

Saturday afternoon is always a busy time at the fruit stand and this one was especially so. Mr. Strievely never left the counter all afternoon, and in spite of the fact that Kate was at his side much of the time, the drive was never free from patrons.

Evening came, and Kate was needed in the house and her father outside. Little did she realize his anxiety, much less her mother's, and she tripped and sang as she served the borders in the dining room. Everyone seemed in gay spirits tonight. Why not? The world was full of gaiety.

At seven o'clock, Kate was dressed and ready. The car was coming down the street. She gave herself one final examination in the mirror, reinserted a few hairpins; tightened her slipper strap and stood at the door. Mr. Strievely ran across the lawn and opened the screen in front of her.

"Where are you going tonight, Kate?" He was a little out of breath.

"Why?"

"I want to know."

"We're going out riding."

"Where are you going out riding?"

"We're going to stop some place."

"How do you know?"

"You always do, don't you?"

"Not always."

"Kate, tell me where you are going, or I'll go down and ask Marty."

At that instant the car stopped in front of the house and gave three honks and Marty opened the door.

"We're going over to Loveland, I think, but we're not going to stay long."

"You're not going, Kate." Her father stood in the door, tall and imposing.

"Not going? And why not?! Three more short honks. The others in the car were laughing and talking. Kate's face and neck grew red in spots and she held her breath behind her teeth.

"Because, it's no place for a Christian to go. I'm ashamed to have people know we allow you to go to such places."

"Oh." Her lips seemed to freeze from the cold word.

"If you can't tell Marty you're not going, I will go out and tell Marty myself.

"Indeed you won't." She caught at her throat with her hands and her lips trembled. "I will tell him myself. Let me out. They're waiting." And she attempted to open the screen, but her father did not move. He looked at her square in the eyes.

"Remember, I said you're not going to Loveland Park. Understand? If you do, Marty Brubaugh won't take you out once more!"

"Oh, *I know he will!*" With a flash of her big eyes Kate dashed out the side door and ran to the car, which was off before she had quite taken her seat.

It was an extremely vexed girl who rode toward Loveland Park. Every inch of the way that spark of anger seemed to set some new cell afire in her brain.

She talked and laughed more than usual and it launched the whole party into a giddy mood, yet Kate with all her jesting, could not deceive the others from the fact she was tense with excitement over something.

Marty was the first to feel it. In fact he sensed something wrong when he saw Kate's father in the doorway and Kate's sudden appearance from the side door. Besides, she had failed to greet him in her usual manner. He said nothing however, but gave vent to his aggravation by driving at a maddening pace toward Loveland. He drove ahead of all but one car on the road and came near upsetting once. When one is "wound up" he often does things he afterwards shivers at.

Once more those exquisite, dancing, dazzling lights! Lights that make you laugh, lights that make you wonder, lights that make you tremble, lights that make you hungry and lonesome and sad. Who can explain their psychological stimulus to the young mind? Combined with the buzz of the ever-moving crowd and the swelling and fading of the never-ceasing music, it produces an effect much like strong coffee to an overly sensitive lady. She cannot resist drinking more, more, yet just a little more; but with pleasure of the stimulant is not lasting. A few hours later, how gladly would she relax in sleep.

There was a larger crowd at Loveland that evening than at the Caverns a few weeks ago. This was a "wilder" place and larger. Even tame people were drawn as if by magic just to see what a reputed "wild" place had to offer. But these three young couples weren't hankering after anything wild exactly. No, it was just the thrill of getting near "wild" people and seeing for themselves the things they often heard about.

Once more the music and the lure of the dance hall held them spellbound. No, it wasn't the dance hall, but the dancers. How loving, how affectionate they acted. Surely this was the heart of Loveland.

"Come on in," called out the man at the entrance. "Room for a few more."

Marty grinned sheepishly and shook his head. The girls lowered their eyes bashfully.

It was late when they started for home. Again Marty drove fast and Kate wondered why. Always on the way home he took his time. He drove and said practically nothing. The four in the back seat talked in undertones. Marty left them off at the front of the Stieverly home. A light was burning in the lower bedroom. Kate frowned.

Ten minutes later they were still sitting in the car, but neither had spoken a word. Marty cleared his throat several times. Kate must go in. She would. She couldn't. She bit her lips and looked toward the strip of light from the room door.

"What's the matter, Kate?" Marty did not look at her.

"Why, nothing. Why?"

"Something is wrong—I—"

"You—what?" She looked at him out of the corner of her eye.

"I know something is the matter. You were not yourself tonight."

"I wasn't? Why?"

"That's what I want to know. What was your father talking to you about when I drove up? I saw—"

"Oh, he just wanted to know where we were going tonight. Her voice was calm and deliberate.

"He objected?"

"Sort'a"

"That's what I thought." He stepped on the starter. Objected to you're keeping company with me, huh? That's what I've always thought. It's all right, Kate; I only wish I would have—"

"No! No! Marty. He doesn't object to you, not a bit, only he doesn't approve of going to Loveland. Don't you see, I—"

"Well, it's alright, Kate. I won't argue the point with him." He sprang from the car and opened the door on Kate's side. Blindly, as a dream, she walked up to the house beside him. The lights and much of the Caverns and park combined, seemed to be jumbled up in hideous wreckage before her eyes.

"Goodnight," he said bitterly, and ran to the car.

"No! No! Why Marty!" she screamed.

***

The bedroom door did not open at her entrance as she feared. She heard not a stir. Softly she went upstairs to her room and without turning on the light or undressing flung herself across the bed.

"Oh! He will. I **know** he will, shouted through her mind a thousand times. "I **know** he will. Oh, no—no. I **know** now he never will. All because father had to—oh dear—"

Kate complained of a headache and said she was not going to Sunday school but her mother insisted, so she went; but she was twenty minutes late and got little out of the remaining discussion. She was invited to spend the afternoon at Dreasers, but declined and would give Lucile no sound reason why. At home she only sampled the dinner and went upstairs immediately after the dishes were done. She never knew before, a Sunday afternoon could be so dreadfully long.

As the custom, she walked to church with her mother, but much to the surprise of everyone, came home alone. Alone---yes alone, and she had seen Marty walk off with Althea Ward, and they were talking and laughing. She saw!

Three days passed. Three months it seemed to Kate. She felt tired from morning to night and was never hungry. She forced herself to do everything and seldom volunteered in the conversation. Did her parents notice it? My, what a foolish, impossible question! At least at the end of seven days, the little mother who found Kate sitting alone in the dim library, touched her gently and said, "Dear, what's the matter?" There was a lingered hesitation.

"Oh nothing," She choked feebly.

"But there is, Kate. You can't hide. What's happened?"

"Oh, everything!"

"I'm sorry Kate. Can I help you?"

"No." A stifled sob escaped her lips.

"I can't see you go on like this and say nothing. What is it dear?"

"I don't know. I don't know any thing." She sobbed. "Everything's wrong—everything! I don't know any—"

"Why, Kate," said her mother tenderly and put her arm across the bent young shoulders. "Why, Kate," she repeated. "You are not supposed to know everything; but you can know one thing, and that is that the Lord understands you and knows all about it and He cares. Yes, He does, Kate. He saves."

Her whole body shook now and then her mother wept silently with her.

"Don't you believe it, Kate?"

"Yes, she whispered."

"Do you believe He wants to help you?"

No answer.

"Do you believe He is able?"

"Yes."

"Do you believe He loves you?"

"Oh, yes, I know He does, Mother."

"Then that's all that's necessary, my dear. If you know it, then live in truth of it. Rest in it, and everything will come out alright."

Mrs. Strievely bent and kissed her daughter and softly walked away, leaving Kate crying.

There was no sudden change in Kate, as might have come to some after such a confession. But gradually she learned to realize the secret joy of believing it. It left a blessing on every attitude of life. Of course, there were days of valley experiences and again she caught herself saying, "I don't know. I don't know anything." Without an exception, the thought of Marty quickened her spells. Then as if strengthened by another power, she could say, "I know how the Lord cares, if Marty doesn't."

It was not necessary for Kate to tell her father she was sorry she had disobeyed him on that Saturday night, for he read it often in her eyes and voice. He had never mentioned it to her. He was very kind.

Althea and Cliff were becoming fast friends and Marty was friendly to everyone and no one in particular—that is among the girls, but there was a friendship growing between the boy and Cliff Marrow. They sat beside each other in Church. They spent evenings and Sunday afternoons together and Cliff even brought Marty to the Bible Study much to everyone's surprise and comment.

Six months rolled by and Kate was six times happier than she had been in six months previous, but almost fearfully, she held her breath and doubted its reality. Early in the spring she was holding her little sister on her lap, telling her a story when the phone rang.

"Is that you Kate?" She all but dropped the receiver.

"Yes it is."

"May I come over to see you tonight?"

"Why, why yes."

"Your father won't object?"

"No, of course not."

"Are you sure, Kate?"

"Why, Marty, I *know* he won't, but I'll ask him to make sure."

DALE'S DIARY

By Christmas Carol Kauffman age 29, Halstead, Kansas
Originally published November 22, 1931
in the Youth's Christian Companion

Nov 11

School closed at noon because this was Armistice Day. Mr. Rowe gave a lecture in the gym on peace. He said the world will be at peace when the majority become civilized, meaning I guess the majority even in the United States are uncivilized yet. We sang a bunch of patriotic songs and Eddie Pratt sang, "Lamar Strangled On A Banana" in all three verses and got us fellows to giggling until we almost got scared. The parade passed the school just as we walked out. Then I came home and helped Ma finish cleaning up the garden and rake and dig up bulbs and etc. I'm sure tired tonight.

Nov 12

Seems like since I'm in H.S. I never get done studying. Every teacher seems to think their assignments are the most important. I spent over an hour in the library on outside reading for history and then didn't get half done and so it was dark when I started peddling my papers. Ma says I better drop my route, but I don't want to. I don't like the idea of a fellow my age asking his dad for every cent. Any way, Mr. Berman thinks that everyone of us fellows ought to be earning something. He's going to take us out hunting Sat. I'm going to give mine to—haven't decided yet.

Nov 13

I wonder why Mr. Thear calls on me so much in General Science? I wonder why I can't think of something too, so Dad could retire and so we could get a decent car, and I could go to Church Academy next year. I'd rather. I have a bunch of ideas I'm going to work out someday. I wonder why Emily B. is looking at me every time I look at her, almost.

Nov 14

It was real frosty this morning and our bacon and eggs sure tasted good. It's the first time I had morning devotion on a rock pile, but I will never forget it. I came home with a half bushel of nuts and torn pants, which Ma didn't like, but I wonder what Skinney's mom said when he came home. "Come let us worship and bow down: let us kneel before the Lord our Maker, is what Mr. Berman taught us this morning on the rock pile. He said he's going to take us back to that rock pile for something special and the one who remembers the verse will get something valuable. I wonder what. I'm glad for once I've got a diary to refer to.

Nov 15

We had a class meeting just before Junior Church tonight to decide what to do for Thanksgiving. I don't know why Jess always has to act stubborn. Ma said that's the way his mother is. Everyone one of us is to give some special Thanksgiving gift to some person and the Thanksgiving gift must be accompanied by a Thanksgiving verse. I can't imagine what mine will be.

Nov 16

The North End State Bank was robbed this noon and the bandits escaped with $3000. Parkie was across the street and saw them leaving in a green roadster. He most always gets to see all the exciting things. I was just five minutes too late.

Nov 17

I caught the first rabbit in my trap last night. I like it better than chicken. Ma said I'd never catch one here in town but facts are facts, so I'm going to try it again. I saw another drunk man tonight. He would have been run over if I hadn't stopped him. I watched him till he got home.

Nov 18

We got a letter today from Uncle Ben and he says he's stopping off here on his way east. I can hardly wait. I wish he'd bring Albert along. It snowed today and we had our science lesson outside because our lesson was on snowflakes. I can't believe there are no two alike. If I ever discover there are two alike I will get my name in the paper. I saw a pair of skates and a set of books in Dottie's window I wish I could get.

Nov 19

We are invited to Aunt Fannies for Thanksgiving and she said if we come, she will have cottage cheese for Dad and spareribs for me. I hope we do. Ma said Aunt Fannie always had a special liking for me ever since I was tiny. Well, anyway, I'm glad I can tell her I've kept up my diary that she gave me even though I don't believe much in diaries. Smith's little Betty got into the medicine cabinet today and spilled carbolic on herself and Ma is over there yet. Ma got supper, which was better than I thought it would be.

Nov 20

I went over to Sanders after supper and heard President Hoover talk over the air. Miss. Miller said I gave the best report of it in class today. Her compliments have been few, so I thought it would be worth writing down.

Nov 21

I cleaned out the cellar today and Martha cleaned out the attic. It's better not to yoke us to the same job because Martha is too slow for me. I found a vinegar jug Ma lost two years ago and she gave me a dime. When a fellow hits his finger with a hammer, how is a fellow supposed to keep from saying something? I didn't say it but I thought about it real strong.

Nov 22

I wish I could have lived when Paul did and been with him in Rome and Corinth and been his private secretary. I wonder why there is no one like him living today.

Nov 23

Pa says were going to Aunt Fannies and Ma wrote her a letter today. I decided to crack my nuts and take some of them to her because she lives alone and has no one to gather nuts for her, and this shall be my accompanying verse: "I will offer to thee a sacrifice of thanksgiving and will call upon the name of the Lord." It is quite a sacrifice, because I'd like for Ma to use them in candy jars.

Nov 24

I got a haircut tonight. So did my Dad. Dad's getting the car all ready too, cause Uncle Fred will be there too, from Ohio, and Aunt Fannies cousin, Ike. I sure like him.

Nov 25

We had a Thanksgiving Prayer Meeting tonight at Roher's. I feel more like Thanksgiving then I never knew of before. It's snowing now. I'm glad Ma put a blanket on the end of my bed.

PS. We're leaving real early in the morning for Aunt Fannies, but not for Thanksgiving. We received word an hour ago that she passed away in the middle of the night, and her neighbor found her this morning. We will be gone several days.

Nov 30

How can it be? Oh, Aunt Fanny, I wish she could hear me thank her. She went and left Dad $3000 and $1,500 of it is to be spent on my education, and I am going to Academy next semester. Dad and Ma both said so, and I am going to tell Mr. Berman tomorrow night.

THE JOYS OF CHRISTMAS

By Christmas Carol Kauffman age 29, Halstead, Kansas
Originally published December 20, 1931
in the Youth's Christian Companion

A cold wind and an icy mist is blowing today, and I am glad I am close to the fire with this little black knitted shawl around my shoulders. It is not mine, but I like to wear it because it is so soft and warm. Some dear old mother must have left it in our house. I have asked every grandmother whom I can recall having been here during the last year. I know it belongs to some grandmother because it looks and feels like it and even smells like it; like dried rose peddles and lavender. I wish I knew to whom I could take it today, for I am sure she is wanting it. Then too, I'd like to sit and talk to some dear old mother all afternoon and just sit and rock and help piece some quilts blocks, maybe.

I've been thinking of Christmas all week, and even though it is two months away, each day I find myself more jubilant over its approach. And each year I find it more so. That tinkling, almost breathless feeling, and awe I used to experience as a child on Christmas Eve has never left me! I wonder if it ever will?

That's why I'd like to be visiting this afternoon with some old mother who has passed about as many Christmases as I have and ask her about how she feels about Christmas this year.

"Well, I can hear her say, "this has been a hard summer for Pop and I, and we can't hand out presents this time, except to the grandchildren, but if we all live and the Lord willing, we'll have all the children home once more. We've never all been together since John's moved south. And now he writes they're planning on coming. If we have all the children home it will make twenty-two in all. Well I 'spect that's the best we can do."

I can see her face light up with a radiance almost divine, and I wish I could catch it and send a snap to each of her children to keep. What a wonderful, what a glorious Christmas she will have, if her dream comes true.

Home! I never think of Christmas without thinking of home! I remember the middle drawer, in the old fashioned dresser, where I hid all my precious (trifling) gifts. Each of us had a drawer and we knew without being warned that no drawer except our own was to be touched, not even glanced at. And those whispers and strange signs Mother and Father exchanged before Father started off for town! How we wondered, with vibrant anticipation. Often we wrote down a list of things we'd like to have and left it lying sorta careless like in some place where we were certain Mother would find it.

And then the stars, the bells, and the wreaths we fixed up in the house! Oh, weren't those happy moments when Mother came from town to find the house transformed according to our childhood fantasies. I'll admit, now, although it would have broken my heart, to have been told so then. It was not always done artistically, but did Mother ever say so, or even show the least intimidation? Never! Never!

"Well now, what have my children been doing while I was away? Isn't it beautiful? A bit early perhaps, but, no, don't take it down."

I do believe I was the first in the neighborhood to put a bell in the window. Perhaps, I have always been over anxious for Christmas to come because it is my birthday, you know.

Then, Christmas Eve at last! The long, longed for eve, when we wrapped our presents, (to this day, the rustle of paper sends a thrill through my body) said our prayers most fervently, gave our kisses a little longer and went to bed. And, long after we were supposed to be asleep, we would hear Mother and Father tiptoeing around below.

Oh, thank God, they never taught us to believe in Santa Claus! Oh, praise God for these blessed, thrice-blessed, Christmas morning worships, when before we dare open a thing, Father read again that beautiful story from Luke (we all knew so well), and knelt in prayer; not exactly as we do other mornings, but always on Christmas morning, each of us, even the baby, offered a prayer in reverence to that holy Christ Child. I can't remember what we prayed, but God does, even as He understood the youngest as we prayed at the table, "Food fer amen" She meant to say, "I thank you, Lord, for the food, amen."

By that time, even the opening of our presents took on sacredness. Christmas has *never* been a time of hilarity for us. I bow my head again in thankfulness for those who taught us differently.

Oh, can it be that parents love their children so? What hours of patient stitching these little gifts manifest! What sacrifice, what love, and what confidence they speak. Disappointed? What a cruel thought! Oh, that during the year we might be worthy of these little gifts which represent only a drop in an ocean of love to us.

A neighbor lady told me once how eagerly she rushed to her well-filled stockings, only to find it filled with stones! Her own father had done it as a joke. Joke! Thirty years had passed when she told me, and even then her eyes filled with tears. "Ever since that day," she said, "Christmas has never been the same." Then I thought how kind, how very kind our Heavenly Father is to His children. Would He ever disappoint one of His little ones like that?

What brings perhaps the happiest memories of all, were our programs in the church. It is a cold Sunday evening. The snow is deep and we start off early; but before we start, we must stand by the door and go over our songs and recitations once more,--twice, if not to Mother's satisfaction the first time. Then she puts her arms around us and kissed us and tells us she will be so happy if we do our very best. Will we? How could we do less?

The church is filled, even the standing room is taken, and many turn away. The singing starts. Those wonderful hymns of the Christ Child, that nearly burst the soul for joy. Everyone looks happy. The visitors join in. What a happy night! I was five when I spoke my first piece, and it gives me joy today as I remember Brother Lambert giving me a nickel for saying it again for him after the program. I wish I had a hundred nickels to give away this Christmas with a "God bless you child," as he gave me. But dearer to my heart and fonder is the remembrance of being folded in my parents' arms, and being told secretly I did my part well. I wish this afternoon I might have the consciousness of knowing that in the years since, I accepted Christ as my personal Savior, that I have put forth as equal an effort to do my part to the best of my ability.

Last Saturday afternoon I looked up from my book with a start. A strange, almost mysterious sensation went though me. My husband was humming "Silent Night."

"Oh." I half cried.

"What is it?" He asked.

"That song! No other song in the world so grips me, so fills me with unspeakable gladness and joy as that one. When I hear it, I see angels and everything Christmas means."

"Really?" He smiled and went on humming and I heard him singing it as he swung the milk pails on the way to the barn.

Oh, that it were possible for every family to be together this Christmas, but I know that wish can never come true. But I pity those most, who could be at home and choose not to be; for instance, the young man who skipped off for a high time, or the girl who left home against her parents' wishes. Can't you see those mothers watching at the door, and crying when Christmas Eve comes and the table is set. And the Son of the Christmas Mother is watching too, tenderly watching and waiting, waiting!

As I anticipate this Christmas, I wonder what it will bring, not necessarily of gifts, but of that which will enrich my life. For most of us it will bring that which we are ready to accept; and this ability to receive is measured by what we give. I, too, as many of you, will not be able to hand out expensive gifts, and that which may cost us much (but not more than we can afford) unto the Creator of Christmas—our love.

Last year I searched quite a while for a greeting to send to an old friend. I was very particular. At last I found it. It was a picture, not of Christmas trees, Santa Claus, nor silly figures (so many are) but of a Baby in a manger, a Cross and a Crown, and below it was this message: May you come to realize the joys of the eternal Christmas." I breathed a prayer as I dropped it in the mailbox, that she would catch the message of that verse, for I was not sure she was realizing that joy.

Yesterday I heard a little boy say he wished Christmas would come once a month. And I heard an older person say, she wished it would never come. What a contrast! When I am old, will I forget the Christmas joys of my childhood? God forbid. Christmas, once a month, little boy?

"I want your love, and Christmas will be yours eternally."

THE STORM

By Christmas Carol Kauffman age 30, Halstead, Kansas
Originally published February 14,21, and 28th 1932
in the Youth's Christian Companion

On the night of this story, the thick red mud on the Pine Valley Road was covered with a crust of ice and a stinging, slanting rain sent a chill to the bones of any man. Teachers dismissed their schools at noon, fathers filled the wood boxes extra full and mothers kept their children in the kitchen and held the tiniest ones close in their arms. Toward evening a howling wind accompanied the rain and all engagements were canceled and programs postponed. What few cars made their way north or south, did it with much struggling and moaning.

The houses on the Pine Valley Road were few and far between and the kerosene lamps inside cast very little light on the world outside. The lights from the Sawyer house were no exception. The blinds had all been drawn but two, and since the house stood well back from the road and was partly hidden by a young orchard, a passerby might easily be unaware of the fact that he passed the house of one of the best known men in the country.

Jake Sawyer was known for his complex character. He was extremely courteous, but could be extremely impolite; very generous and decidedly stingy; jolly and stern, energetic and lazy, affectionate and cruel. Upon first meeting him one was impressed by the first-mentioned characteristics only. The other Jake Sawyer came to be known upon better acquaintance, or it was whispered around at quiltings and public sales. That he was the subject of the neighborhood gossip, was unknown to him.

Madeline shifted uneasily in her chair, gave a swift glance in the direction of the clock and bent closer over her work. She could hear two clocks ticking, one on the paper-draped shelf above the table and a dollar alarm clock on the windowsill in the bedroom on the left. They were not in step. The alarm clock was out-ticking the big clock and it made Madeline nervous. She had a notion to close the bedroom door. She would just as soon as she finished that seam. But then that door had such a merciless loud squeak, and always caught on the old dog and cat rug. She would let it open. The clock would not make her as nervous as that door.

Why didn't Uncle Jake oil that door? He never seemed to notice anything that needed fixing. The rag carpet by the door fluttered, rose and left with the rising wind. Madeline moved her chair back and rocked jerkily.

Squeak, squeak. Oh, she was on the loose board in the floor. It had always been loose as long as she could remember, but it never squeaked as loud as tonight. A gust of wind set the window blinds a-flutter, and flung several loose shingles against the side of the house. Faster and faster she worked her needle and all but bit the pin in two she held between her teeth. Her scissors fell to the floor with a crash and she was glad no one saw her jump. If she really was nervous she did not want anyone else to detect it. She was cold, but she didn't want to go after what? That noise—bang! Madeline held her needle in mid air and caught her breath. Bang again!

This time Aunt Mollie heard it too, and turned her head abruptly. She was sitting close to the stove, just sitting. Not a word had been spoken by either till then. The gray-haired woman turned a sad face toward Madeline and said: "I wonder what that was." The next time she heard it she leaned toward her husband, who had slid to an awkward position on the end of his spine, his big feet under the stove and his chin resting on his chest, fast asleep.

"Pap" she called. "Ho, Pop." But the man made no answer. She took hold of the man's knee and shook him vigorously.

"I say, Pap!" This time she was able to produce a reluctant, "Huh?"

"Did you latch the hen house door tonight—Pap?"

"Huh?" he squirmed slowly. "Now Pap." She shook him again. The old man roused himself and rubbed his face.

"What did you say, Mollie?"

"I say, did you latch the henhouse door? Listen it's a knockin', Pap. You can't hear it with such a wind a blowin, then what will be left of it till mornin? Those poor hens!"

The woman was on her feet now and came toward Pap as if she would pick him up bodily and set him on his feet. Slowly as a schoolboy walks to his corner of punishment, Pap Sawyer "moseyed" towards the door.

"Well, I 'spect that means I'm supposed to go out and see, eh?" He reached for his lumberjack. "S—funny it had to happen on a night like this. Sounds like it's makin' weather outside." He pulled his cap well over his ears and lit a lantern. As he opened the door a sheet of icy rain drove him back a step. He backed out and slammed the door.

Madeline hurried to the window and looked out. The night was black as pitch. She could see the old man faintly in the light of his lantern. Slowly he measured his way to the end of the walk. Several times he slipped, regaining his footing and skidded on across the yard. Fido let out an unearthly howl and sprang to his master's side. Madeline shivered. This time the woman noticed it.

"Is it gettin worse outside honey?"

"Oh, its awful, Aunt Mollie. The yard looks like glass."

"This is the way it started out twenty-six years ago this spring, when Pap an' I seen that awful blizzard come on."

"Oh!" Madeline picked at the edge of the curtain and looked up anxiously. The clock on the shelf clamored ten. "Oh!" The cry that rose in her throat died there. Ten o'clock. Would he never come? She had been waiting since four. Five, six, seven, eight, nine, ten. Ten! Six hours of waiting, agonized waiting. Yet she tried desperately to hide the agony.

"Do you really look for him tonight, Madeline?" The woman's voice was tender and anxious too.

"He said he would be here, Aunt Mollie— at four- at four! I think every minute I will hear the car, but I hear every other sound but that one. I hope he didn't start out if it was like this at home. But—but then He'd never make it. She sighed and looked out into the storm. The rain was turning to sleet and shot against the windows like hail. Now and then a big white flake came with it.

"He doesn't know, Aunt Mollie." The girls face was pinched and tense. Her voice was near a whisper and she gave a hasty glance in the direction of the hen-house.

"I hope not, Madeline. You may be sure he did not learn it from me. You're all packed ain't you, so you could leave right away?"

"Everything is ready. But if he would come now, yet— Oh. It's so late—and the roads—"

"I knew I latched the henhouse door—'for I went out," growled Jake Sawyer, as the door burst open. He placed the dripping lantern and made tracts of mud across the room to the stove.

"What was that noise then?"

Pap had a way of evading questions when he felt like it, and he felt so inclined tonight

"Must be someone sick down at Bechers," He put in.

"Why so Pap?"

"Seen a car turn in there."

Madeline started and then caught herself.

"Anybody'd be a fool to go out on a night like this, except for sickness or death, or a weddin' and a weddin could be postponed."

Madeline Strickler had been working for the Sawyers since fall. Three weeks after her arrival she started calling this man Uncle Jake, much to his pleasure. He now noticed a strange look in the girl's eyes and saw her fingers twitching nervously.

"You aren't scared of the storm, are you, Madeline?" He asked tenderly. She had won a spot in the old mans heart.

"No Uncle Jake," A sweet voice replied.

"You don't look like you felt the best, somehow. You're not takin cold are you?"

"I don't think so." She said this in a weaker voice.

"That must a bin' doc' Gibson's car I seen turn in. It came from the west."

"It must be one of the twins again," put in Aunt Mollie. Seems like if it ain't one, it's the other or both. Poor Mrs. Becker, I'll call her up in the morning."

"Why not call her up tonight yet?" The doctor ought to be leavin' in bout half an hour at the most. Maybe I ought to take Madeline down there." Jake Sawyer was piously rubbing his hands as he made this suggestion. It was exactly the same kind of hand rub Deacon Brown used when he made his public appeals for the poor fund.

"Mary Becker might just be needin someone", he added still rubbing his hands.

It's 'most ten thirty Pap and it's half a mile down there. It's a wonder you seen the car through this storm."

"It had most powerful headlights. Thought I heard a funny noise as it turned the corner, but I couldn't a seen whether it went on, on account o' the hedge. There's so much noise goin' on outside tonight, I couldn't make right sure o' no sound."

Jake Sawyer still had coat and cap on and a pool of muddy water surrounded his booted feet. If he had been in any one else's house, he most certainly would have thought of removing his boots. He may have thought of doing it even in his own home, but he did not always obey his conscience here. Aunt Mollie made no mention of the things that sorely grieved her, for she had long since learned it was of little use and only added to her sore of disappointments. After all, man's greatest failing is not stupidity, forgetfulness, nor even absent-mindedness, but plain thoughtlessness, and in the case of Jake Sawyer, it was often intentional.

"What say, Madeline," he said presently.

"Shall I call up and if they need you--- say I'll take you down?"

"Oh." Faltered Madeline shyly and the color rose in her cheeks. "Oh, really I don't believe I could tonight," and she gave Aunt Mollie a meaningful look. It was not like Madeline to shrink from any service, great or small, and Uncle Jake was not a little perplexed at the answer.

"How would you ever get her down there, Jake?" Put in Mrs. Sawyer. "You won't ever take the car out in such weather to go to church."

"This is different. When a body's in trouble it's only Christian to act neighborly. I could take her on Bessie."

Madeline turned toward the door. She thought she heard a car coming. But it must have been the wind playing havoc in the attic-way. The clock struck ten-thirty-- ten times thirty nerves in the girl's body started creeping, twisting, jerking. Oh, she hoped now he would not come till morning.

But how could she go to the bed and sleep? Sleep was the farthest thing from her.

"Madeline has worked hard today." Aunt Mollie said, "and I think she ought to go to bed right now. An' I think we all ought to be goin' to bed."

Now it happened that Jake Sawyer would do anything to find favor in the sight of the Becher family. His finest manhood was exhibited towards them,---his kindness, his generosity, his keenest affection for, was not the Jake Sawyer thus known throughout Pine Valley? And he meant to keep up his reputation.

He removed coat and cap and after sufficiently warming himself, he walked to the phone and took down the receiver. Madeline bit her lips to keep back the tears. Oh, she simply could not go down there tonight, no matter if both twins were desperately ill. The chances were, he might come yet.

"Sam?" Jake Sawyer's kindest voice sounded over the wire. "Some one sick down your way?" I went out to fix the hen house door and saw a car turn up your lane. Thought no one but a doctor would be goin' in your way a night like this. What say? Accident? Benton?

Madeline was still standing near the window. She thought she screamed, but no one heard it if she did. She swayed for a moment, then caught hold of the edge of the table to steady herself. Her face, as well as Aunt Mollies was white with terror. The voice on the phone was dry and husky. The rough hand of Jake Sawyer grasped the wall for support. The voice at the end of the other end of the wire was still talking and the voice of Jake Sawyer was saying nothing, only breathing heavily and grunting now and then. His collar grew tighter around his neck and the muscles in his face twitched angrily.

"Yes, he snapped sarcastically, "She is. Yes sir—" (long pause). Jake Sawyer's face paled to the color of the ashes in the stove. Aunt Millie made her way to Madeline's side.

"I'll see," and *click* went the receiver.

Like an angry dog ready to pounce upon a crippled animal, Jake Sawyer turned toward the two women with misty wondering eyes, in the corner; their arms around each other.

"So?" he roared coming near with clenched fists. "So you thought you could deceive me, did you, Mollie Sawyer?" He grabbed her arm with his paw-like hand. Mollie made no answer, only grew yet whiter and struggled for breath.

"Answer me, Mollie." He demanded, and his eyes shone black and glossy. "Did you know your brother was coming here tonight?" Answer me, I say!"

"I—I wasn't sure, Jake." She whispered between sobs. Madeline sank suddenly to the floor on her knees, buried her face in her arms and almost as suddenly sprang to her feet and hurried to the bedroom and the big man sprang after her. With trembling hands the girl was working herself into her coat. Her boots were on the floor beside a suitcase.

"And what have you to do with a lowdown scoundrel like Fred Hepler? He was standing in the doorway, one hand on each side of the casing, penning her in like a helpless bird.

"Oh, I have everything to do with him, Uncle Jake." Madeline was surprised at the steadiness of her voice, much more it surprised the man she addressed. Like a sudden unexpected calmness in the middle of a storm, a quietness of soul passed over the girl. Now, at the most trying moment she had ever experienced, she humbly faced the man she had feared the last few months. The God of Strength, to whom she had been praying, seemed to be standing at her side, now supporting her, and she was unafraid, though this was the first time he had ever displayed anything but courtesy toward her.

Madeline—ah, Jake Sawyer would have done anything to please Madeline, and she knew it. But Madeline also knew there was another Jake Sawyer. She looked up at him with pleading eyes.

"Is—is he really hurt, Uncle Jake?"

"Not as bad as he would be if I had a hold o' him." His eyes looked wicked and she could feel his hot breath on her face.

Mollie let out a stifled cry, "Oh Jake!"

"Shut up! You know what I always said!" And he reeled on his heels.

"I know Jake, but—but you see he didn't come here. God prevented it."

"God? Who thinks He did? And he can thank his lucky stars. He tried to come here." (He waved his big arms in the air) "And you women planned it. Sneaks, cowards, hypocrites, —HA!" He let out a hideous laugh. At the same time the house shivered and rocked with the angry wind, and the dog let out another weird howl. "But what I'd like to know is, what relation this young lady is to that hobo of a—"

"Stop!" cried Madeline. "He is none of that." And instantly she was at the door. So beside himself had Jake Sawyer been with fury, he had not taken notice that Mollie was putting on her wraps too. He stared at her as in a nightmare.

"Oh, you think you'll take a little walk this beautiful evening?" he sneered.

"It would only be Christian to help our neighbors in trouble, reminded Aunt Millie as Madeline opened the door.

Both women expected a remonstrance from the man, but he made no move to prevent them, only stood there and laughed at them in his gruesome manner.

"Then go." He grinned, "and let Satan go with you. And remember, Miss Madeline, as long as you have any relation whatever with Fred Hepler, you can't come back here."

"Very well, Uncle Jake." And two brave hearts stepped out into the storm.

"Madeline," whispered Mollie, as she slipped on the icy walk. "The lantern."

"Never mind, Aunt Mollie, I have this," and she drew a flashlight from her pocket.

"Oh, we must hurry. What if he is dying?" Again a terrible fear seized the girl and every nerve in her body twisted with pain. Hand in hand they made their way down the hill, facing the sharp blades of sleet, stumbling, twisting, stumbling until their feet were bruised, but never stopping, half running and seeming to make little headway as one does in a dream. Neither spoke, neither cried, but the heart-language of the one communed, and both communed with God.

The little mother came to the door. The smallest twin was in her arms. She looked frightened, but as the women stopped into the light of the room, and she saw their mud-covered feet and legs and dripping clothes, she cried, "Ye didn't walk down?"

Madeline nodded. The man on the cot moved slightly and moaned. Sam Becker was sitting at the side washing blood from the man's forehead, and a bloody towel lay under his right arm.

"The doctor didn't get here yet," whispered Mrs. Becker.

At once Madeline was at the man's side on her knees beside the cot, stroking his forehead, his face, his hands, weeping softly and whispering. Aunt Mollie stood close by.

"Daddy," She called softly, "Daddy, are, are you hurt much? Daddy, this is Madeline, Daddy."

The man on the cot lifted his left hand to the girl's shoulder and half opened his eyes and—

There in the doorway, hatless, coatless, dripping, stood Jake Sawyer.

***

No one had heard him come. No one had heard him enter, yet there he stood, like a ghost, huge, grim, with a wild expression in his eyes. The man on the cot roused himself a moment and stared. Every face turned toward the object of his attention. A deathly silence fell over the room. Mollie, white as a sheet, fell at the feet of the man—her brother.

"Uncle Jake," Madeline was the first to speak, "don't do anything to disturb Daddy now."

Like one insane, Jake fixed his gate on the group, now on one, now on another, never moving a muscle of his body.

"Daddy?" She muttered. "Daddy?"

Another silence, almost deathly, fell over the room. The man on the cot moaned again and Madeline kissed his hand passionately.

"Take a chair, Jake," spoke Mr. Becker, motioning to a rocker, but Jake did not seem to hear. He was watching the form on the cot and the expression on his face would be difficult to describe, so changing, so complex, it was. Now tender, now brutal, now wondering, now defiant, now wild, now human, now childish, now dazed. Mollie watched it, and held her hand over her heart.

"He skidded into the culvert," Mr. Becker exclaimed. "Spose you noticed the car when you came in the lane. Just comin' in with water when I saw the lights and heard the crash. Went down an' brought him in."

"He walked up?" Madeline asked.

"Yes, didn't seem to be hurt much till he got inside. Sorta keeled over then. The heart, I guess. Called for you right away, Miss Stickle. Said he was comin' to fetch you for a weddin."

"Gladys is getting married tomorrow. I—I was to be her bride's maid." Madeline shook now with sobs. We can't ever make it now, and poor Gladys, I wonder—he was to have been here by four."

"Said he had car trouble."

Fred Hepler was not unconscious as he lay on the cot. He heard and realized everything, but somehow could not talk yet. He wanted to tell her not to cry. He wanted to tell her how he had left home in plenty of time. He wanted to tell her that he would soon be alright and they could start back soon—but the car—it was still nosed in the culvert, one wheel off. His head—pain—his arm was heavy—yes he would soon be alright—but he was sick—dizzy—rain—mud—gutter—sleet—mud—windshield—lights—crossroad—mud—on and on he drove in one long dream. No wonder his arm ached. They both ached. His head too—and his throat. Yes, Jake! The man roused himself again and tried to lift his head—too—and his throat—oh yes Jake! The man roused himself again and again tried to lift his head. Jake was still standing in the doorway.

"Jake," Fred Hepler reached out the hand Madeline had been kissing. "I didn't quite make it to your place, but you didn't come here to kill me, did you?"

The heart of Jake Sawyer stopped beating a moment. His mouth fell open and he made a heavy lunge toward the rocker. The most painful thing that can happen to a man of pride is to have his other self exposed to the man in whose sight he wishes to find the most favor. For a moment he felt a more stringent pain than the man on the cot.

"He is talking out of his head, Sam. Too bad."

Madeline and Mollie looked at each other, and Fred looked at Mollie.

"Pap," said Mollie in a clear voice, and she got to her feet. "Pap, I've stood for a lot since I married you. You caused me grief and pain no one ever heard about. But for once, Pap, I won't keep still and hear you try to cover up your deeds. You know you threatened to kill my brother if ever he came near the place, an' you know you haven't let us write to each other these fifteen years or more, an' you needn't act so surprised to find out now they took Madeline to raise. And when Miss

Madeline Strickler wrote to me for work, why should I tell you she's my brother's daughter, an' why should we tell you he's comin' to take her home to see her sister's weddin'. Pap?"

The woman was crying now. "I loved you when I married you, an' I've loved you all these years, and I never told a soul about how you quarreled with Fred that night after the sale and threatened to take his life, and I'd never of told it now if you hadn't driven me to it. You followed us down here to do us harm, an none of us'll raise a hand in self defense, 'cause we all know you're strong as a giant when you're mad, an' we all know you're as lovin' an' meek as Moses when you want to be. An' I'm goin' to tell you now, Pap, that Beckers have known all these years somethin' was between my only bother an' you, cause he's sent my letters here, an' Mary slipped them to me. Yes, Pap, twice a month Fred an' I've been writrin, to each other an; I've known from the first, Fred's took little Madeline to raise. So you got scared and jealous tonight when you heard Fred Hepler called for Madeline Strictler. He's done a good job so far, don't you think, Pap?"

Jake Sawyer shed many a tear at funerals and when he spoke words of sympathy to the bereaved, never before did he feel tears, but today the tears of shame came to his eyes. He brushed them away quickly with his coat sleeve. He opened his mouth but no words came. He looked at the floor but there was no hole to hide him. Tears of shame are not always a sign of repentance. That his good neighbors Sam and Mary Becker should bear such a testimony from Mollie, was almost beyond endurance. But more poignant than this, was the consciousness of the girl Madeline that brought sunshine into the home, the girl that had renewed the old time sparkle to Mollie's eyes, the girl he had learned to love as his own daughter, knew— knew he hated this man, her father, yet never intimated that she held the least accusation.

There she knelt beside the man she loved as her real father, beautiful, delicate and womanly. Slowly something from the black, stubborn bosom of Jake Sawyer, struggled to be free. Some strange power seemed to soften the strings of steel that bound his heart.

Other tears came, not only of shame, but suddenly of a broken heart; broken for sin.

"Fred." The big man came toward the one on the cot. Mollie—Madeline, it has all been over nothing. Can you forgive?" The door opened and in stepped the doctor. He could not understand the mysterious light that seemed to fill the room. It was if a divine fire glowed from the eyes of each within. Jake Sawyer followed him to the door some minutes later.

"Do you think he will be able to be taken to the early morning train, doctor? There's a wedding at noon. His daughter and that young lady will be the bridesmaid."

"Oh, I think so," he said after a little hesitancy. I'd venture quite a bit to be at my daughter's wedding. How far?"

"To Benton. My wife and daughter will go along an' take care of him.

LITTLE MAMIE'S OWN SELF

By Christmas Carol Kauffman age 30, Halstead, Kansas
Originally published April 10, 1932
in the Youth's Christian Companion

Little Mamie is exactly eleven years old, that is all. A new and wonderful thing has just taken place in her young life, and in a few weeks she will be received into the church by water baptism. She is the third in the family of five children, and somehow, strangely different. Mamie's own mother cannot always understand her, and who else can, but her guardian angel! Would you like to have a glimpse into little Mamie's own self? No one else ever has, for truly it has never been told because there was no one to tell.

In School---"Oh, I wish I could all at once vanish—go right through the wall without making a sound and be at home in my own room or all alone in the big empty church, only it wouldn't seem empty with You so close to me, Jesus. Maybe I could study my lessons better there—there where I was sitting last night when You lifted me up and I felt light as a feather. I can't read my lesson here today—Marcella laughs so much and keeps asking me what's got over me. I can't make her understand—nobody can, but You, Jesus. Oh, I feel so warm and happy inside, and that song keeps singing itself here in my heart. 'Calling today, calling today.' I feel sleepy, yet not exactly. I can't think enough here. Now it's two o'clock already, soon it will be four, then Marcella will walk home with me. I'd rather be alone. I will go to the library a while and read— no I will look through that big art book again and find that picture of Mary. Oh, she is so sweet. Could I ever be like her? This lesson. 'The gold-headed dragon jumped from the cliff into the'—I wouldn't be afraid of even a dragon—not any more. Anyway this isn't true, but Peter walked on the water. And that's true—deep water, but You caught him Jesus. I wouldn't be afraid.

"Snowing? How big and white and light, and they all fall so softly. I wish I could be out in it, and get all covered with them. Snowflakes come from heaven, way up there beyond the sky; but You can see right through snowflakes and clouds and houses.

"I wonder what You thought last night in church when I went forward? You seemed to smile upon me and take away all my sins. Now You'll never remember I told Johnnie that lie---two lies, and took Alvin's penknife, and cheated in spelling. I'll never do it again, no, never. I don't feel like I'd even get cross at Bertha, not even if she'd make a 'snoot' at me like she did yesterday.

"What did Miss Stephens say? "Fifth grade reading"—Oh, I don't have my lesson. I couldn't today. Will she punish me? Can't she understand? I can't tell her. She is so queer. But, I have always had my lesson before. I will stay after school and try to explain—the dragon with the golden head—"

After School---"I wonder if Mother will be worried because I am coming home so late. It isn't so late and it was so nice in the library. It is always quiet there. I am glad Marcella went along. So she is going to the dressmakers tonight. She has such pretty things. The dress is old—used to be Verna's, but I like the way it is made, and the red braid. Father said it makes me look like a lady. I am one—almost. I am almost as big as Vera, and have so much hair. I can do it up, maybe. I wonder why I feel older now. Mr. Waters talked to me like he did to Oprah, and she is fifteen. He said he was sorry he didn't see me stand up. I felt like crying then. It's dreadful to stand up and not be noticed; but you did Jesus, and I stood up for you.

It's almost getting dark. What did that boy call? Extra papers? What is it? The president died? But, Oh, maybe he was glad to. I wouldn't be afraid to die. It must be nice and cozy. And heaven must be beautiful. I suppose, of course, he went there right away. I wonder how it really happens. I suppose the angels come and get you right away.

There is Mother on the porch. She is getting the paper. She sees me coming. She asked me last night if I understood the decision I made and really meant by it that I wanted to be a Christian, and be baptized. I said "Yes", I wish Mother wouldn't think I am such a little girl, even if I am small and cry when I get hurt, and play with dolls once in a while. I'll always like dolls, even if I'm seventy. I wish I could sleep alone tonight. I wonder if Vera felt like this the day she went forward. I think I will always be like this, but she isn't; but she is a good girl. I wonder if Mr. Rogers will shake hands with me tonight. I hope Mr. Johnson stands up tonight. He looks so sad and that would take it away. I can't think of anything that will ever make me sad again—not sad for long."

At the Supper Table--- "I like to sit her next to Father. He seems to love me so and understand. Maybe he—Oh no. He was never a girl like me. But maybe boys feel like this too after they do it. But Father was almost twenty. I heard him say so once. The President. Everybody talks about how awful it is. Why is it awful? It is if your not—Oh, I took too many potatoes. I didn't think—I was not very hungry tonight. Maybe I won't get very hungry any more. Then I will get thin and never grow. I will try to eat anyway. This fresh bread is so good, so is the gravy. In heaven we never get hungry, but Mrs. Grimes said the cookie jar would always be full. That will be for poor children who never had enough. "Why does Joe have to pick at me because I am so quiet? They always called me chatter-box and 'snicks-snoots' and now when I am still they tease me. Joe doesn't understand either. I wish he didn't look at me so. I know Father understands. The tears try to come when he touches my hand that way, but I don't want to cry 'cause I'm not a bit sad. I will hurry and do the dishes right away and tell mother to go and get ready. She looks rather tried. I wonder if she was like me one day. Now they are coming already to practice that song. Vera has a pretty voice, but Thelma spoils it. Thelma acts as if she doesn't like me; I don't know why. Oh, I am glad Father said he would help me do the dishes, and Vera is glad too. We can easy do them in fifteen minutes."

In Church---"I think Mr. Walters is good looking. I wonder what his little girl looks like. She must be pretty too. I wonder how it would seem to be a preacher's child. I think it would be wonderful. I don't suppose you'd ever feel like being bad, and everybody would love you. I guess everybody always loves preachers. I do anyway, almost always. He is looking at me. Does he expect me to give a testimony? Oh, really—I—never did—I can't hardly—nobody would understand; and Mrs. Dibley is talking now! She always talks too long. Now Mr. Tremer, and Sally Smith, and now he is looking, I—I—oh, he is calling for a special song. I couldn't have done it really, for trembling. Maybe he understands. You do anyway, Jesus. It's not that I was ashamed. Maybe tomorrow I can---just a verse. I'll have one ready. "John 3:16' I'm glad he chose a text that I can find easy. He said I should always carry my Bible, so I will. I am glad it is all my own and has my own name on the front. If he would ask for Bibles up tonight, I would raise mine high. I don't understand everything he is saying about incarnate and Deity, but I know it's good. Father said the preacher was 'smart' and knew heaps about the Bible. Who-so-ever---I know that. I am one of them. 'Believeth'—I believe, why I always believed, always. I wonder if I used to be saved and didn't know it? I wish I knew. If I was lost I should have been most scared, but I wasn't ever, very. They are singing that same song again. I almost wish I could stand up again and go forward. Oh, Mr. Johnson, please stand up. Jesus please help him. There—there he did; and now he looks happier already. And Mrs. Johnson is crying so. He is asking for everyone who hasn't confessed to come forward. This means me too. I am glad. Will he shake hands with me again? And it helps me so and he seams to love me and I am only eleven. Mr. Benson never seemed to. But Mr. Benson will surely now, if I go to his instruction class. Olive Creyer is coming, too, and Mrs. Stoner. He stole fathers axe, but Father will easy forgive him."

In Bed After The Light Is Out---"Eleven or twelve, which did it strike? I am not sleepy yet. I wonder how it would seem to be to be awake at night. The night I broke my arm, I must have been. I wonder if I will ever get it broken again. What if I got run over and got smashed, or the house got on fire and we all got burned? Once some people did. A whole school of children burned. Did You do it Jesus? Did You let my arm get broken when I fell? My feet are cold. Vera is asleep, but I am glad she is here with me after all. She doesn't know I am awake. I am glad it is moonlight. I wonder how close my 'watching over me' angel is? Here in the room? I wish she could come and sit on the edge of the bed and hold my hand. I wonder if it is a girl my age. I wish I could talk to her. Just whisper and Vera wouldn't hear. I'd ask her lots of questions. Maybe she is a big girl and she could take me in her arms and fly away with me. I wonder how it would seem to fly. I like to dream it; only I wake up too soon. What is that? Mother is coughing again. I hope she doesn't get sick. I will pray. You can hear me just as well in bed, can't You Jesus? I will pretend I am kneeling, kneeling on Your knee with my head on Your lap. I can almost feel Your hand on my head. I do love You,

Jesus. It seems I always have, but I know I didn't always try to please You. I will pray till I fall asleep and You will understand why I left off."

You will hear about Little Mamie's own self some other time. Her experiences are not always smooth and rose-scented and no child's born-again life is, even though they are only eleven years old.

MOTIVES FOR EDUCATION

By Christmas Carol Kauffman age 31, Halstead, Kansas
Originally published February 7, 1933
in the Youth's Christian Companion
written for the Hesston College Journal

Never before in the history of the world have there been so many students enrolled in educational institutions as today. The modern pursuit of knowledge, of better schools and school systems is demanding payment of millions of dollars annually. The call of the world is for more educated men and women of learning. The church calls for more educated men and women to carry on the work—men and women with, not only a good education, but a willingness to do it for the service of the Master. Our own church schools as well as other colleges and universities and a call for more workers is also becoming greater. One of the saddest and most challenging— is the fact that some of the most promising and educated young people are not helping to carry on the work of the church. Did their motive for work and education lack in purity and loyalty to their calling? If the nature of our students in our three church schools would be that the natural powers God has given them and the harmonious development of all their facilities be fully consecrated and increased for the service of the Master, I believe the work of the church could be carried out one hundred percent better than it is today and the church of Christ greatly enlarged.

I would like to develop this subject from that standpoint. First the value of having determination for an education, the value of having an unwavering aim; and second having a clarity of motive in the Christian ideal. Henry Van Dyke said:

"Life is like an arrow, therefore I must know what mark to aim at and how to use the bow. Then draw it to the head and let it go."

The most important thing in the mind of the individual seeking an education is to have a great aim and then to process the aptitude and perseverance to attain it. A double minded man is unstable in all his ways, but a man with an aim who sticks to it is the one who succeeds. One great purpose is like a great magnet for it attracts all the abilities to that purpose. To succeed we must concentrate all our faculties in our minds upon that one motive. Scientists estimate that there is enough energy in fifty acres of sunshine to run all the electricity in the world if it were concentrated, yet the sun might blaze out upon the world forever without setting anything on fire. There are students of great ability in our church schools, when it is concentrated on an ideal. Chiseled on the tomb of a discouraged heart broken King, Joseph the II of Austria in the royal cemetery in Vienna is found this epitaph: "Here lies a monarch who with the best of intentions, never carried out a single plan." Many of us have good intentions, but do not possess the perseverance to attain them. The student who comes to school with one unwavering aim for his education, and who sticks to that aim is the one who wins, whether that aim be to preach, to teach or to farm.

On the prairies of South America there is a flower that always inclines in the same direction. If a traveler looses his way, and has neither compass nor chart, by turning to this flower he has a safe guide upon which to rely, for no matter how the rains descend or the winds blow it's leaves always point to the north. I have seen students who remind me of this flower, for their aims are so constant and their motives so well known, that no matter what difficulties they may encounter, or what opposition they may meet, we can tell almost to the certainty what they will some day accomplish. It is the motive that gives meaning to an education and individuality to the student.

Saint Paul's power lay in the power of his purpose. "Let thine eyes look straight before thee. Ponder the way of thy feet and let all thy ways be established. Turn not to the right hand, nor to the left." Nothing could doubt; nothing could frighten Paul. The roman emperor could not frazzle him. The dungeons could not appall him, no prison could suppress him, and obstacles did not discourage him. The student who says, "This one thing I do and this one aim for my education, I pursue," is the one who will win. The young woman whose aim is to become a musician will attend the school where she will get the best training along that line; the student who wishes to become a doctor will thoughtfully plan his educational career, and the one who's sole aim is to serve the Lord in some definite way, will seek an education with a motive to that end.

Motives, however, may vary, but to the Christian they must be always good and pure and tend to develop not only the physical and mental but also the spiritual life for the influence of good. "Jesus grew and waxed strong in spirit, filled with wisdom, and the grace of God was upon Him." Paul told Timothy what should be the Christians motive for learning when he said, "Study to show thyself approved unto God, a workman who needeth not to be ashamed, rightly dividing the word of truth."

When Gambetta, that great republican leader of Marcellus, started off to school in Paris, his mother bade him goodbye and said, " My son, try to come home a somebody." For three years he lived and studied in a dingy little garret and went to school in shabby clothes, all because of his ideal and loyalty to his motive. He was one day chosen by Jules Farven, when he was sick to make his public speech for him. That night all the newspapers in Paris were sounding the praises of the ragged uncouth Bohemian boy, and before long he was recognized by all of France as the Republican leader. This sudden rise was not due to luck or accident, but to loyalty to the motive that his education should bring to him or to his mother.

When I left home my parents did not tell me that, yet I know they were praying for me every day that my education would bring honor to the Master. Many of you have parents that are doing the same. I was very much impressed with the address that Professor Weibe gave in Chapel and I wish to repeat one statement he made. "Get an education, get all the education you can, and then use it for the service of the Master." The ethics of education today is strong in habit, but weak in motive, strong in standard, but weak in spirituality. Any life work or study that paralyzes or harms the spiritual life in any way should be avoided.

Our motives for an education should not be for title, or riches or honor, or social pride, but to honor the Lord who gave us our abilities. The tendency of the age is to expend its genius in perishable arts, but the education of Christian manhood and womanhood is above all riches and overtops all titles. The development of Christian character is greater by far than any career. We should first of all study for ourselves and find out what God has fitted us for and then seek an education with the sole aim of filling that place. Power and constant growth toward a higher life are the greatest end of human existence. The world is full of men and women who are almost a success, but not quite, like a great machine not quite completed. Perhaps some of us students are almost a success in our Christian experience, but not quite, because not every desire and every ability is in full sympathy with our calling. We must give our lives, our energy, our enthusiasm to all the highest of which we are capable. There is only one real failure in life possible, and that is not to be true to the best we know. It is of great value to have a motive, and to the Christian that motive is good and pure. Our motive for an education then should be just the same as the motive for every other act in life, that all our abilities be fully consecrated and increased for the service of the Master.

—Hesston College Journal.

DALE'S DIARY

By Christmas Carol Kauffman. Age 29, Halstead, Kansas
Originally published November 5, 1933
in the Youth's Christian Companion

Sept 9

At last my dream of many months may come true. I hold my breath. But for Aunt Fannie it would be impossible. Pa was called back to work today. N. R. A. Seven months out. He seems different already. He said tonight I may go to school, and insists that I must go to our own school. I'd be happy to go to high school but Pa usually wins in a debate. It is Aunt Fannies dying wish and that is what the money is to be used for, but I am not sorry I made Pa borrow some this summer. What would we have done? I'm going to think for a while and then go to bed.

1:30 no sleep yet. I ought to wait another year and help Pa.

Sept 10

Now Ma says too I should go. Martha does nothing but listen and blush. Mr. Berman knows about the money, but I've never told the bunch. Wonder what they'll say, especially Tim. Ma's getting my clothes together. She says they will get along, but I don't see how. Mr. Berman had the class at his place for lunch. I like his wife OK. Pa and I drove down to the depot after church to see about trains.

Leaving tomorrow at 5:50 or 8:30. PM. Excited.

Sept 11

9:30 PM An hours ride from home. Just ate and apple. Train
rather empty. Moonlight. Men all talking Cuba. I think I'd like
to be a conductor. Next time he comes around I'm going to ask
him a bunch of questions---maybe. He didn't look like the answering kind. Wonder what the folks are doing. Ma looked
tired. She had the whole class over for supper. Everything
planned. The fellows gave me a dandy notebook. Martha was
extra nice, I thought. I believe Phil likes her. He'd better watch
out. I gave my paper route to Parkie. He's the "whitest" negro
I ever knew.

Sept 12

3 PM--- Just finished discussion with the man across the isle.
Said he had no use for church schools and said I had was a
fool for going and a lot more "blah" I'm not going to mention.
Offered me a cigarette. Made fun of me. Three boys at the end
going to state college took out hip flasks. The conductor asked
me if I had one too. When I said no, he slapped me on my
back and said, "Keep away from that stuff young man. If you
know what all I see on the run, you'd be fed up for a lifetime."
Just finished reading the letter Ma said I should read before I
get there. Wonder if those fellows ever had a mother who
cares like mine does. Ma's lunches are swell, only there isn't
enough. Gives a fellow some appetite to ride all day.

7:15 PM--- Saw some sights earlier today. Anxious to get out
and run. Must fill out the card Ma stuck in my Bible. What if I
hadn't opened it on the hour she told me to? Really, this diary
is a nuisance, but whenever I think of Aunt Fannie, I've got to
keep it up. So long, old train

Sept 13

Some things not at all as I expected. Many folks ordinary like myself. Roommate Ben Krebbiel from up north. German and not too handsome but jolly. His first year in academy too. So we have much in common, even heart failure at the table. How some girls can stare. Haven't left the table stuffed yet. Good grub, what there is so far. Our room looks as bare as a chicken without feathers. I introduced myself ofener today than in all my life so far. Don't understand why they didn't name me Raymond or Edward or something more dignified. Ben doesn't keep a diary. Don't blame him. Students had a mass meeting tonight. Remember only three teachers names. "Professors" I should say. I feel green.

Sept 14

Now for study. Think I'll like every class. Had a letter from Ma today. Said they miss me at the table. Played ball at 4:30. Got beat. Ben and I purchased a few necessities for our room. Looks better. Quite a town. Some fellows have their own cars. I landed a job at the hardware store on Saturdays. Appeals to me first rate. If that Somers doesn't show up, I may get a job sweeping our halls. Most of the fellows name their rooms. We named ours "Bendale Roost. Ben's not so dumb with the pen. They had a get acquainted social tonight, but I don't feel acquainted with any one yet. Didn't have enough ice cream. Some fellow they call Rastus, carries a camera with him all the time—caught me today just as I spilled an armful of books on the dorm steps. Hope he never prints that. Starting to rain.

Sept 15

Do I like it here or don't I? Took a hike with Alison Roberts. Think we'll be pretty good friends. He's a senior, but not a bit stuck up like some. Wish I had a voice like his. Got a package from home. Things Ma forgot to put in a box around popcorn. There was preaching tonight. The preacher knows Pa. Therefore he said he knew me at once. Ha. Must tell Pa.

Sept 16

I like my job. I got $1.50 more than I expected. My sales amounted to $16.73. I must make out a study schedule. The matron let me have lunch in the kitchen after work. Some of the fellows don't have much for her, but she's OK.

Sept 17

Mr. Berman beats this Sunday School teacher. Biggest crowd in church that I was ever in. Dinner was very good. About half the students gone home. I wrote the folks answering all Ma's questions and a few more. Alison sang in a quartette at the hospital and took me along. I was so surprised. Don't see why he'd pick on me unless he pities me. I don't want to be pitied. He asked me to go to boys prayer circle. A lot of fellows don't go. I took Ben along. Some fellows were there that I was surprised to see.

Sept 18

Well, Summers hasn't showed up yet so I swept the halls this AM. Gave me a ravenous appetite for breakfast. That cook knows how to make pancakes. I visited a literary society against my own wishes, but how these girls can persuade a fellow! I'd join if I could sit and listen, but speaking before a crowd is not my line. Rastus has the mumps. I hope some one takes his picture. Tough luck!

Sept 19

Of all the things to keep a fellow busy! Tried out for chorus today. I couldn't understand the professors grin. At least I was accepted for better or for worse. Ben and I were called down for laughing during study period. Wish we cold get outside and roar.

Sept 20

These teachers know how to make a freshie get down and dig. No time to write any more tonight. Cold.

Sept 21

A missionary from China gave a talk in chapel today. Wouldn't care if he'd talk every day. John B. had his arm broken. Fell from the chimney. Against the rules to climb it. One of the girls has mumps now. Sauerkraut and dogs for supper.

Sept 22

Ben had a birthday today and he was treated at the table. Wonder if they'll remember me with the same kind of stuff. I'm going to get him a cheap diary so I won't have to sneak around to get mine done. He's just Dutch enough to keep me company, I think. His sister isn't bad looking. Had a good game of ball tonight, meaning we won. I was asked to read in devotion tonight. Hope I can get over this weakness of fearing a crowd.

Sept 23

I had the misfortunate of dropping a large pitcher in the store today after a woman customer looked and looked and didn't buy. Oh yikes! Price $1.50. I said I didn't want to take my pay, but Mr. C insisted. Made me feel cheap. I'm going to send the dollar to Ma. Wish I could do more for the home folks. Someone in town got married tonight. Some fellows are going to skip after bells and go serenade. Don't know whether to or not. Hate to be called a "goodie."

Sept 24

Only three fellows down for breakfast and we felt out of place. Some of the girls whispered and giggled till it made us half sick. Wonder what's in the air? Some of the fellows look at me and grin. A few said it was OK. I asked Alison and he said he didn't know. Wrote Pa—not about that though.

Sept 25

Got a letter from Mr. Berman. Dean held all the boys after school tonight concerning the serenading Saturday night. The fellows didn't get in as easy as they got out. Ben was home that night and Alison didn't go, so I don't know the particulars yet. Glad I didn't go. They "raz" me but I don't see through it yet. Doesn't bother me though. Visited another literary. Better. May join someday. Wrote my first theme. Subject: "My Ideal Man" Berman of course.

Sept 26

Was called to dean's office tonight. The bridegroom was there and landed in on me. I was dumbfounded. Declared I had no part. Wasn't out of the dorm that night. Then he handed me a package and handed me my shirt to prove it. Got it in the struggle. I own the shirt---has my name on it. He was sure angry and all the things he told the dean about the bunch I'm leader of. Called me a liar. The dean kept me after he left. Couldn't tell if he believed me or not. He was almost kind. Told Ben. Have a headache. Suppose it's all over school. Who got my shirt? Wish I knew. But I wish a lot more the dean would trust me. Hurts.

Sept 27

Thank God for Alison. He's my true friend. Played tennis. Then took a walk. It's all over school. Sure hate it, but nothing to do but tell the truth. Hope Pa and Ma don't hear about it and Mr. Berman. O God help me!

Sept 28

Didn't go to dinner today. Stayed up here to pray. I felt happy all afternoon. Had a letter from Martha. She's a dear but I couldn't tell her. Glad she's making good grades.

Sept 29

In devotion tonight Mack made a statement. Confessed he came to my room and borrowed my shirt while I was working. He said he was not in the gang that serenaded the bridegroom. His statement sounded genuine and after church he shook my hand. Several other confessions were made. I never was in such a meeting before. The dean gave me a look I'll never forget. I felt sorry for Mack. I'm his friend for life—just give me a chance to prove it. Don't think I'll tell the folks for a while.

TOMMY

By Christmas Carol Kauffman, age 29, Halstead, Kansas
Originally published December 3, and 10, 1933
in the Youth's Christian Companion

Tommy came in late again! It was the third time that week. And this was Friday. Pale-faced and starry- eyed, he walked quickly to his seat and glanced at no one, not even the teacher. Tommy knew he was late, for the sixth grade geography class was already reciting. The people did not need to remind him with their imprudent tattletale grins, and mocking sidewise glances. Red spots appeared on each pale cheek and his breath came to fast for him. He had run the last half-mile, for when he reached the top of the hill—oh—to his horror, he saw that the playground was empty and he was tardy again.

Tommy felt big Jason's piercing eyes bore at the back of his neck. He would find out why Tommy was late so often. Sure he would. Tonight after school he's sit on Tommy until he told, then report to Mr. Daniels. It would take a hero to find out what none of the other pupils knew, not even the teacher. That sure would bring Jason favor from Mr. Daniels enough to pass him to the eighth grade.

"Each to his own work!" Mr. Daniels snapped his finger. "You need not come to class Tommy. You may receive your geography lesson to me alone at recess." Big Jason coughed boldly without necessity and little Violet looked sorry.

Tommy answered Mr. Daniels with a look, not of fear or disappointment, but relief. Strange. Again the teacher could not understand.

And wasn't that usually the way with this Tommy Tucker? Half the time Mr. Daniels could not understand Tommy's actions. He had not met up with such a child in all his five years experience in the hills. Some teachers might have called him queer, unreasonable, eccentric; but to Mr. Daniels he was simply wonderful---full of wonder. Tommy would say and do the most unexpected things; but not once had he been caught in any kind of misdemeanor or had been called upon with his lessons unprepared. Tommy was the brightest pupil in school and he received the grades he deserved.

But this thing of coming in late was getting the best of Mr. Daniels' patience. It was happening far too often. If it were Sam, he'd give him a whipping. If it were Violet, he'd stop and see her mother. If it were Christopher, he'd make him stay an hour after school—but Tommy, he— well—he just wasn't the boy to be flogged and scolded. Mr. Daniels weighed the matter all morning.

Just as there are no two faces in the world exactly alike, so are there no two school boys hearts that could be unlocked with the same key.

Recess came. And recess at the Cedar Hill schoolhouse was something every one of the eleven boys enjoyed, especially this time of year, for it was spring in the earliest awakening. Flickers called in trees near by; tiny snappy buds were appearing on the big maple; squirrels chattered; a gopher scurried away; a lone violet bloomed along the creek, half hidden by the comfort of old leaves. No one spied it there.

The youngsters whooped and yelled with astounding lung capacity. Even little Violet laughed joyously. Caps came off and shot over the schoolhouse roof. Boys climbed trees to get a deeper breath; Girls sat on the dinner bench and wondered how big the world was, how far the sky, and wished that recess would last forever. Mr. Daniels wished for something of that kind for himself. His head had a dull ache, and he wanted to be outside with the children.

"Come to my desk Tommy," Mr. Daniels voice was positive, but not harsh. Tommy obeyed.

"It's too nice to stay inside today. I would like to get out for a while." He was not looking at Tommy, but out the window. "You may recite to me after school."

"But Mr. Daniels—I—can't."

"You will anyway."

"At—at the last recess, oh, please, but not after school."

The boy looked frightened. His lip quivered and he looked his teacher square in the eyes. Something like a prayer was written there, and without another word the teacher walked toward the door.

"Very well, Tommy. See that you do that."

Should a pupil obey the teacher or should the teacher obey the pupil? Never before under any circumstances would Jess Daniels have given way like this. He was shocked and ashamed of himself. The very idea that he should take orders from a sixth-grade Tommy, who couldn't get to school on time! All the children shouted and ran—all but Tommy. He got a drink and sat on a log behind the coal shed; just sat and looked at the hill. Jason made his way to the corner of the shed several times and showed his crooked teeth. Tommy made no response. When the last recess came Tommy walked to the teacher's desk with his book under his arm.

"You have your lesson?"

"Yes sir."

"Did you have it this morning?"

"Yes sir."

"I'll take your word for it then. Now, why were you tardy again?" This is the third time this week."

"I didn't leave soon enough."

Mr. Daniels bit his lip. "Look here, Tommy, why didn't you leave sooner? Answer me at once!"

"Well, I didn't know it was so late. I—I kept on working."

"Working at what?"

Tommy's eyes fell and his shoulders sagged. He fumbled the pages of his geography nervously.

"Answer me," Mr. Daniels put a hand firmly on Tommy's shoulder. It shocked him that it felt so boney. The boy shook.

"Are you sick, Tommy?"

"No sir."

"Do you feel alright?"

"Ye—Yes sir."

"What do you do?"

"Everything—I mean most everything."

"For instance?"

"Well, I—I—"

"Hello Tommy Tardy." It was big Jason who stuck his head in the door. "Come out and play Tommy Tar—"

"Jason, come here!" Mr. Daniels voice was sharp as a razor and Jason obeyed, sheepishly dragging his clumsy feet over the doorstep.

"What d'you want?"

"You may stay after school is dismissed for acting discourteously."

"I didn't do nothin', I was jes—"

"Excused. Not another word. Stay as I tell you."

Jason went out like a whipped dog. Now his fun was all off. Tommy would be over the hill before he got out. At the door he looked back and gave Tommy his blackest look.

"Now listen Tommy," the teacher continued, "You've been tardy three times this week and I can't have any more of it. I've never allowed it other places and I won't allow it here. It's bad for the school and it's bad for you. Were you tardy last year?"

"No sir."

"What would the teacher have done?"

"He would have whipped me, I suppose. He did the others."

"Do you want me to whip you?"

"You can if you like." Tommy never winced a muscle.

"Are you used to being whipped at home?"

"No sir."

"Well, I don't like to punish, but I may have to—Tommy, see that you watch your clock on Monday morning."

"We have no clock, but I will try to be here on time, sir," Tommy's voice was almost a whisper.

"If you have no clock, how do you expect—"

"I go by the train whistle in North Bend. I didn't hear it this morning. Mother has a watch but it doesn't work any more."

It was past time to ring the recess bell, but the teacher did not notice. He had noticed something new—something strange about Tommy's eyes, a suddenly familiar expression that made him catch his breath and look away. He had never noticed it before and this was his seventh month at Cedar Hill. He looked again. What absurd thoughts! Yet, was this why he cold never be severe with Tommy? The cedar hills themselves were mysterious and filled of wonder. Why shouldn't the children who came out of them be filled with wonder, too? Jess Daniels could not give a reason for his attitude toward Tommy Tucker, only admit that he was the strangest and most difficult to understand pupil he had ever had.

Every now and then that afternoon the teacher caught himself looking at Tommy. Somehow he got through that Friday afternoon's schedule, but the face of Tommy followed him down the spelling book, across every copy book, and all the way to his boarding place, and stayed with him will into the night—those big, gray, hungry, deep-set eyes.

Dogs seldom tell secrets. That's why Tommy told Gyp everything. And that's why Gyp loved Tommy.

"Look here Gyp," Tommy's voice was almost a whisper and he got his face close to Gyp's and held his arm around his neck. You stay right here by the window and watch. And if she lifts her head like this, you come out to the shed as fast as you can. OK Gyp?" Gyp looked at Tommy and licked his slender wrist affectionately. "Now you stay right here where you can see her and don't take your eyes off that window. Understand Gyp?"

The dog blinked a dog's, "Yes." Tommy gave the dog another to-be-certain glance, patted him several times on the head and ran to the shed.

Several boards of certain lengths lay across two old boxes. With difficulty Tommy sawed a forth and fifth from what seemed to be an old gate. His arms trembled and more than once he wiped away blinding tears with his soiled shirt-sleeve. Several times he stepped to the door of the shed to see if Gyp was keeping his promise. The dog had not moved from his place and his eyes were on the window. Tommy worked until nearly sundown, and Gyp did not call him. But, more than once the dog beat the ground with his tail when he heard Tommy hammer. Twice he heard this young master make a sound like a stifled cry and shook in desperation to dash to him, but devotion held him to his post.

"All right Gyp. You're a good Gyp. Best old dog a fel-low ever had. I'll see if I can get you something to eat."

Tommy staggered to the door. A ten-year old boy ought to be half starved after a job like that at which he had been working, but Tommy was not hungry—not for anything to eat; but a gnawing hunger, far greater and more poignant than most boys have ever felt, weakened Tommy to the point of near exhaustion.

"Oh, Gyp," the boy flung his arms frantically around the dog's neck. "It won't be long now. It's nearly done and yours—won't take so long." He sobbed. "Sh, be quiet now when we go in the house. Stay here by the door." Gyp, as always obeyed and asked no questions.

Tommy tiptoed into the next room. The setting sun hanging low behind the Cedar Hills filled the room with a pinkish glow and put a delicate tint on the white face of the woman lying there. Tommy touched her face, half-frightened, wondering.

"Tommy," she whispered. Her eyes opened.

"Do you want a drink?"

"No."

"Milk?"

"No."

"Anything?"

"No dear, only you. Is it about finished?"

Tommy nodded, for he could not answer. More than one thing was breaking the heart of this boy who, but a child must act the part of a man. It does not seem fair that circumstances bring nothing but happiness and play to some and to others work and disappointment. But that is the unchangeable difference of destiny. If I ever were you and you were I, would God be any more just? This is a question that has baffled the soul of many a boy less fortunate than Tommy.

In the month just past, Mr. Daniels had read in school the life stories of four great men that in their boyhood had desperate struggles with hardships of every description. But Tommy, boy-like, and human, couldn't think of being very great just now.

"Have you had your supper?" The great heart of any mother would have asked this even at such an hour.

Tommy shook his head.

"Is there anything left?"

"There was a little baloney and I gave it to Gyp. And milk. There are eggs."

"Go eat Tommy."

"I—I can't."

"Do it anyway, dear. Be brave, and God will help you. I can't stay long any more now, Tommy. I am anxious to go. I have told you all. Do everything as I said. The letter is on the dresser. Take it just as soon—" She did not finish, but opening the Bible, which lay at her side, asked Tommy to make a light and read once more the fourteenth chapter of John. Tommy had read it often in the last two weeks and could do so without hesitancy.

***

"Goin' away, Mr. Daniels?" Mrs. Dyke looked up from her scrubbing as the teacher entered the room, hat in hand.

"Yes, Mrs. Dyke, I wonder if I could use Ginger for an hour or so?"

"Well, now I spec so, teacher. Be ye goin to town on such a cloudy Saturday morning?" asked the overly inquisitive Mrs. Dyke. "If ye be, I have ye fetch me along a sack of cornmeal bein Jake might not be gettin to town till next week,"

"I hadn't planned on going in to town, Mrs. Dyke. But I'd gladly bring it for you if I were. I'm going down to the school over the hill to see one of my pupils."

"Well, now, who might it be ye goin to see over the hill? "There's the Samuels but they ain't got a youngins in school yet, and the Cooks children is all growed up."

"I have a Tommy Tucker in the sixth grade and—"

"Tommy Tucker, that's right. Now, he's some boy, I'll bet, ain't he? I jes bet ye got yer hands full with him. Officers came and got his father soon after they moved in there, and we heard he died in the pen three years ago come this spring. Some said his real name ain't Tucker, though I dono about that."

Mr. Daniels chin dropped and he headed himself toward the door. "Do you know any more?" He demanded.

"Not a thing, Mr. Daniels. We never got ourselves out of the neighbors with such and I guess the rest of the folks feel 'bout as we do an knowed. But I heard said, the mother and lad are harmless, but I dono now. Ye may be a welcome caller, an again, ye may not be." She continued her scrubbing with a chuckle.

"If I shouldn't be home by noon, go ahead and eat without me."

"Well, I hope ye get back safe."

Mr. Daniels had some difficulty in finding the place from the road. He was determined not to inquire of anymore. Twice, he followed what appeared to be a lane not often used, but both times it lead to the same place, an old corral in a beautiful valley. Half a mile in the distance, hidden almost entirely in a clump of trees, stood what might be a house. He turned Ginger quickly to what might be a house and was soon close to the first tree. He stopped abruptly, crouching behind two closely set cedars. A pony beside him was Big Jason, fierce eyed and startled.

"What are you doing down her Jason?" Jason stood up and made a snickering twitching grin.

"I—I came over to help you out Mr. Daniels." Jason's face reddened and he fumbled with his cap.

"Help me out? How's that?"

"I'm going to find out for you why Tommy comes tardy." Mr. Daniels drew his horse so close to Jason, he jumped back.

"Get your pony this minute, Jason Redman, and get home as fast as you can. I'm taking care of this matter and I don't need your assistance. Go!" Without a word Jason mounted the pony and struck off across the valley as fast as the animal could take him. Mr. Daniels watched him until he was out of sight. Not once did Jason look back.

Slowly Mr. Daniels neared the house. It was as he imagined, a small, battered, weather-beaten place. Once probably white or gray. A handsome German police dog sat below the west window, his gaze fixed intently on something within. He did not jump up as dogs usually do, but with one quick glance at the shed, barked twice. Instantly, Tommy was at the door and at the same moment saw the teacher dismounting at the gate. He dropped his hammer in surprise.

"Doing some carpenter work this morning Tommy?" Asked Mr. Daniels smiling.

Tommy answered only with a sigh. A shadow crossed his face.

"Let me see what you're making. Maybe I can help you?"

Mr. Daniels placed a strong hand on the boy's shoulder, and he felt the goose flesh over his arms.

"Tommy!" His clutch tightened on the boy's frail shoulders. He clasped him with his other hand. The perspiration came to his temples. Across two old sawhorses stood a box approximately five and a half feet long and two feet wide, crudely made and pitifully rough at the corners, but carefully lined with a beautiful white quilt. On the floor beside it was a half completed box of smaller dimensions.

"Tommy—what is that?" Pointing a shaking finger at the lines box. There was little chance for a mistake. It hit Tommy like a bolt when Mr. Daniels asked. Tommy's eyes were blinded with tears.

"Why? Why?" he choked. It's—It's—a casket for my mother." He was sobbing now.

"Tommy, Tommy, What do you mean? When did your mother die?"

"She—she didn't yet." But, she said maybe today." The man made a low tone as if in terrible anguish of soul.

"And that?" He pointed to the other box.

"Gyp—for Gyp." Tommy was shaking convulsively now. He would have fallen had not his teachers arms held him.

"Who's Gyp?" he demanded.

"My dog. I couldn't take him along."

"Along to where?"

"Why, to the orphans home, you know," Mama said there's no other place for me. He could hardly speak. She had a letter written."

"You're not alone here?" Tommy nodded.

"And this is why you have been tardy lately and couldn't tell me? Tommy you're my hero. Hot tears fell on the boy's head.

"I had to get it done."

"Let me see your mother." Tommy reluctantly turned toward the home.

"Come Gyp." The dog wagged his tail. Instantly he leaped to his master's side.

Hours—weeks seemed to elapse before Mr. Daniels reached the room where they young woman lay, eyes closed and gasping as if in pain. She stirred as the two entered the room and opened two large, gray, deep set eyes.

A mass—a jumbled mass—of memories, hazily mingled with years of remorse and prayers of anguish stood like a giant before the man. His hands were like ice and his face on fire. Scarcely could he control himself.

"Ella!" He took the slender hand in his. "Ella, is it really you? I've been searching—for—twelve years." He was white around the lips.

She smiled faintly. "You have?" Her voice was weak.

"Tell me you forgive me. Oh, Ella!" he choked. "All these months so close, and did you know?"

"Yes, Jess. That's what's—killing—me."

"And—and Tommy!" All the while Tommy was looking on with wondering eyes, as in a dream.

"No—I—never could tell. "The letter, Tommy, give it."

From the dresser, lying on the open Bible, Tommy handed his teacher a sealed letter. It was dated a week before and addressed to Mr. Jess Daniels, teacher of Cedar Hill School. He tore it open, trembling, and read:

Dear Jess:

I have known from the first it was you. I asked Tommy everything. I have never told him because I want him to respect and obey his teacher. I have had nothing but sorrow since the day you ordered me from the home and said you would never again own up to your sister. I lived to find out Jim was a rascal and fugitive from the law, but he loved me in a way. I never told Tommy what his father did. I've tried to teach my boy the way of God, but I will not live to see him a man. I am dying of a broken heart, but I have made all things right with God, and am anxious to go. I've told Tommy to give you this letter as soon as I'm gone. You don't have to own me as your wicked sister, but only as Tommy's mother, and in the name of Christ, notify a decent lawyer to come at once and take care of Tommy. The cow and chickens and other things I think will bring enough to pay him and send Tommy to Bellplane Orphanage. I don't care where I'm buried. All I care about is Tommy. He always has been a good boy. I would not trouble you this much, but I know no one else in the Hills. Jim died three years ago. I have gone by the name of Tucker ever since we came here. Tommy never knew any different. Tommy made my casket. I knew I couldn't afford a real one. I forgave you long ago.

Ella

The man dropped on his knees beside the bed, and with Tommy and his long-lost sister, gathered them in his arms and pled with God in language that could not be written, to strengthen the mother and spare her life.

"Tommy," he spoke tenderly, "make a towel wet and lay it on her head. I'm going to town as fast as Ginger can take me, and will be back as soon as possible with an ambulance." He felt her pulse. She only smiled and Tommy stared.

"Be ready to go along, Tommy."

"Along where?"

"With me." He was leaving without his hat. At the door he called back over his shoulder, "And Gyp can go along too!"

DALE'S DIARY

By Christmas Carol Kauffman, age 32, Halstead, Kansas
Originally Published February 18, 1934
in the Youth's Christian Companion

Jan 5

It certainly makes it interesting with so many short Termers here. How I wish Martha could have come. Went skating to-night. Kitty sure is a jolly girl.

Jan 6

Ben and I each found a rabbit in our traps along the hedge so we had a special table tonight. I gave my first extemporaneous speech today, which was "punk." Clear and cold.

Jan 7

This was about the lonesomest day I ever spent, but I couldn't tell why. Nearly every one was invited out and so I took a hike by myself which wasn't very interesting. A minister from California preached. It was different and appealed to me.

Jan 8

I have been here three months now and can truly say it is good to be here. First impressions are not always lasting. Had a long chat with Alison in his room. He is a wonderful friend to me. That alone is worth being here. He has a way of showing a fellow his faults without making him feel like a pinhead. He reminded me again that I use to much slang. I'm going to try to cut it—I mean stop it. Had a nice letter from Martha. Wish Pa didn't get those headaches.

Jan 9

A genuine blizzard. It is great. Chili soup suits me fine. A bowlful wouldn't go bad right now. Uncle Ben will be here tomorrow to begin a series of meetings. I can hardly wait. He is my favorite uncle. Must get up at five to study.

Jan 10

The trains were two hours late today, so Uncle Ben got here only half an hour before church. He ate supper after his sermon and I ate with him. He says I have changed so since he last saw me. I asked him if it was for the better or worse. He smiled and said, "You're on the right track, my boy." I am glad he has decided to stay in the dorm. He said he wants to have a personal talk with every student. I don't know how that will work, especially with some.

Jan 11

Bad roads. Only a few out tonight. Uncle Ben gave me a package he brought from home. Ma has a heart of gold. I do not deserve it. Played basketball after supper. Close game. If I were home I would have earned a little shoveling snow. Quite a commotion in Girl's Hall tonight.

Jan 12

Uncle Ben spoke in our Literary on the "Ups and Downs of Life." How can a man be so droll and yet be so serious? I like it. I heard to girls say. "Isn't he too cute for words?" What a crude expression. Alison said, "Dale, your Uncle is a man of God."

Jan 13

I got Gid Thornton to work in my place tonight so I wouldn't miss. Roommate called home. Father sick. Still snowing.

Jan 14

Meeting for young folks this afternoon. A number stood. One was Max! He always made fun of anything religious. Alison asked to sleep with me tonight. He is coming now.

Jan 15

I shall never forget this day. It marks the beginning of something new in my life. Something I can't explain, only a vision of the highest ideal in life. Alison made me see it. He talked with me until morning. I know I am only a dense awkward boy, but I want to be a man, a man after God's own heart. "Lord help me! I want to be what you made me for. I want you to help me overcome these selfish, foolish ideas I've had about myself. Help me to be more myself than I expect of others, and all the other things Alison had made me see." I am anxious for a talk with Uncle Ben.

Jan 16

Ben did not come back. The roads are open. I hope his father is not worse. I miss Ben. I certainly fell in love with his folks over Christmas vacation. I couldn't have had a better time any place else but at home. I will write them a letter. I am gong to talk with Uncle Ben tomorrow afternoon at four. A card from Berman's saying they have a little boy named James.

Jan 17

I was not disappointed. Uncle Ben is wonderful. Yet he is very common and even poor, but there is something about him—he has a power; the Spirit of whom he speak so much. I guess he thought some of my questions were simple and childish, but he did not make me feel small. He said he understood, for once, he asked the same things. He told me things about myself I didn't think anyone knew, but he said he used to think the same things. Can it be? I am surprised that the students seem anxious to talk with him. I saw Max go to Uncle Ben's room three times. I never saw such a change in any boy. I don't know how Uncle Ben does it, but he makes folks feel as if he really cared and wanted to help them enjoy their Christian life to the full. He missed his dinner to talk with Mack. Mack is one of my best friends. Would do anything for me.

Jan 18

I have decided to join the volunteer band. Alison spoke to Uncle Ben about it. I have always been interested in missionaries and their work, but since I am here and since Alison has become my personal friend I have an altogether different attitude. Something calls me and I must obey. I wrote and told the folks. I can hardly wait for their answer. I am younger than anyone in the band but Uncle Ben says I am not too young. He talked to the Volunteers tonight and I was there. I am happy.

Jan 19

Ben returned today and seems so sad. His father is better but he says he will have to quit school at the end of the semester. Very sorry. He must go home and do the work. They can't afford a man. Sure hate to see Ben leave.

Jan 20

Let Gid take my place again. Large crowd out. Several confessions. One and old man. I often hear he was a menace to society. I overheard a conversation a while ago, Charlie went to bed early with a sore throat and asked me to fire the furnace for him. The business manager and Ben's cousin were in the storeroom and I heard. I wish something could be done.

Jan 21

I was taken to the Band this morning. All the members accompanied Uncle Ben while he conducted a street meeting this afternoon. Did I ever see so many hungry faces? Prof. B. gave a wonderful testimony. So did Alison and several others. I saw two men in church tonight who were on the street. The offering tonight was nearly $75.00. Had a good talk with Ben after supper. No, he doesn't know, I'm sure. I wrote his mother a letter

Jan 22

I was a terrible student today. Have too many other things on my mind. Now for some solid study. The boys had a special table tonight across one end of the dining hall. Uncle Ben is boy enough that it makes us all love him.

Jan 23

The Short Termers had a special table for Uncle Ben today. He leaves tomorrow. He said he never worked with a more appreciative bunch of students. Ben said he had a good long talk with him. Told Alison what I heard from the furnace room.

Jan 24

About a hundred students took Uncle Ben to the depot. I am thankful for such an uncle. If God ever makes me a preacher I want to be as kind and sympathetic and understanding as he is. Good letter from home.

Jan 25

I had a letter from Ben's mother today. She said I should go ahead and write. I will just have time to get an answer by the time this semester closes. Have a notion not to say anything to Ben until I hear. It would be too bad if it doesn't go through. She seems to have confidence in me. I really am surprised.

Jan 26

Pretty good program tonight. Ben sat beside his sister. She's almost beautiful.

Jan 27

Parkie got my letter today, I suppose. Wish I could see his face. It may not appeal to him. Maybe it was a wild idea and I'd be better off if I left my fingers out of it.

Jan 28

A bunch of us tried a street meeting this afternoon. Good crowd, I thought. The hardware store was robbed last night of about $200.00 worth of guns and tools.

Jan 29

A letter from Parkie and he says he will come immediately. Great! His folks said OK. I am loaning him the money to come on. Told Ben! Was he dumfounded. Ha, he is going home for a few days before Parkie gets here. I am going to meet him and take him out. It will be a splendid opportunity for Parkie and he said he is glad to work for his room and board and clothes. I thought he'd be. Tough luck at home. Auntie said Ben can stay in school. Oh, I hope Parkie will be satisfactory. He *must* be. I'll keep in touch. I'll see that he gets up here once in a while and Alison will be his friend, I know. Parkie, The Lord bless you! I have much to tell you of what happened since I last saw your black face. I didn't tell Ben that I heard his cousin say his father would never get well. Maybe he doesn't know, at least I'm not going to mention it or he'd never come back. And God can change a thing, too.

HELEN'S PROMISE

By Christmas Carol Kauffman, age 32, Halstead, Kansas
Originally published March 25, 1934
in the Youth's Christian Companion

It was during the Christmas holidays that the family moved into the Hobson place across the alley. Helen sat by the dining-room window and watched. A van backed up to the side porch and two men unloaded, not too carefully, the various pieces of furniture. Why handle, with care the shabby patched-up stuff?

"Here," called out one to the other, tossing a red high chair towards the door, "I'll guess that's the last of the junk!"

Then a car drove up. And a half-grown boy was driving. Out jumped a small boy, two, three, girls of in-between sizes, and a bigger one! Last came a mother with a baby in her arms.

"Mother," said Helen, "I do believe there are eight children maybe nine—in such a small house. I wonder so much who they are and where they're from, and there's one girl about my size. Shall I go over and see tonight?"

"Well, I'd better wait a while, Helen, until they get settled. I'm glad it isn't cold today. There comes a little smoke from the chimney now. I'd send you over with a kettle of soup and some of these fresh doughnuts if I knew it would be appreciated."

"But it's nearly two now. They surely have had their dinner."

"I suppose so. A person never knows how much to do for such people. I'd offer to go over and help straighten up if I knew I'd be welcome. It might insult them. Some folks are touchy that way."

It was several weeks after the moving day and Mrs. Wills hadn't been over yet. She noticed that the clothesline

177

had baby things fluttering on it every morning soon after breakfast. And not only baby things, but brown and black stockings in small boy's sizes, little girl's dresses and dishtowels. There must be lots of dish washing, bed making, picking up, and mending for a family of that size. So Mrs. Wills stayed at home and visited from her window, for she might keep the busy mother from her work.

Once she was all ready to go over, and then she discovered the mother scrubbing her back steps and decided not to bother her. The father left early and returned about four, and Mrs. Willis didn't exactly like the idea of calling when the father was at home.

Helen and Gertrude were pretty good friends by the end of the third week. They were both in their second year of high school. Helen had invited Gertrude several times to go along to Sunday School with her but she had always offered the same reason why she couldn't: that on Sunday morning she got up and made the breakfast and did up the work so her mother could sleep longer and catch up on her rest. Once she did go along to evening services and said how much she enjoyed it.

"Gertrude," said Helen on the way home Friday evening, "won't you go along to church Sunday night?"

"Helen, I'd love to. Maybe I can. But I wish Mother could go once. I don't believe she's been to church in three years."

"Doesn't she want to go?" Asked Helen.

"I believe she'd go if she had a dress fit to wear. Aunt Mollie sent her a piece of material for Christmas. It isn't expensive but it's pretty, but I don't know when mother would ever find time to make it. She just dreads to get at something like that for herself. I wish I was handy at sewing and could make it for her."

"Well—well," Helen hesitated, "Maybe you and I together could get it made. I don't know a lot about sewing, but I make my own clothes and Betty's and—"

"Oh, Helen, really—do you think we could?" Mother would be so tickled."

"Is she hard to please?"

"No. Oh, girl, I wish we could do it sometime soon."

"Let's do it tomorrow then. I'll come over as soon as the work is done up. I'll get up early and try to be over by 8:30."

"Helen, I can't tell you how glad mother will be. But she has no pattern. Can you cut one without?"

"No, I'll bring one of Mother's. Something simple and easy to make. Do you have a machine?"

"Yes, an old rattle-trap."

"I don't care how bad it rattles, just so it sews. So long. See you in the morning."

Helen hurried home to tell her mother, wondering what she would say, half afraid she had promised to do something she wasn't capable of doing, yet hoping she could, praying God would help her.

"Mrs. Willis smiled and made no answer. She got out her pattern and carefully explained it to Helen. "And if you get stuck, you can call on me, you know. You won't need to bake the pies in the morning. I'll make pudding and we'll do without pies this Sunday."

"The phone rang. It was Elsie asking for Helen.

"Say, Helen, I'm going to have a taffy-pull here tomorrow afternoon; just our class. My cousin is here from Louisiana and I want to show her a good time."

"I'd like to be there, Elsie, but I'm afraid I can't this time, I—"

"Can't?"

"I promised I'd help a neighbor sew."

"Sew! Oh all things! Since when are you doing sewing for other people?"

"I never did anything like it before, Elsie, but I promised and I really couldn't back out."

"Is that necessary? Can't your mother or some one else do it?"

"Maybe so, but I promised, you know, and I've got to go. Thanks for the invitation. I'll come next time, Elsie."

"Sorry you won't be there then!" I was especially anxious for Marcella to meet you, and you're good at taffy, and seems to me you could do that sewing next Saturday."

"Well, I'll see, Elsie. But I'm afraid I can't be there."

"Well—" Elsie's voice came over the wire faint and hurt like. The receiver clicked without a good-bye.

Helen spent a terrible evening. Elsie was one of her best friends and now—she was hurt and disappointed. She imagined herself at the taffy-pull talking, laughing, eating and having a gay time. Who didn't have a good time at Elsie's home? And she had so often heard of Marcella and hoped some day to meet her. She had a notion to run over and tell Gertrude she couldn't come till next Saturday. She really owed this respect to her Sunday-school class. And if Gertrude's mother went without a new dress this long she could go just one week longer. But then—then that happy look on Gertrude's face when Helen said she would be over in the morning.

"What shall I do Mother?" Asked Helen. "Nothing is too small to take to the Lord."

For a long time Helen stayed on her knees beside her bed. Softly, from below came her mother's voice singing as she rocked the little one to sleep,

"Tis true, O yes, 'tis, true,
God's wonderful promise it true,
For I've trusted and tested and tried it,
And I know God's promise is true."

"Oh, Lord, I want to be true," whispered Helen. "Show me what you want me to do." She opened her Bible and read this verse slowly, "The Lord is not slack concerning his promise, as some men count slackness, but is longsuffering to us, not willing that any should perish, but that all should come to repentance."

Over and over she read, "'The Lord is not slack concerning His promise...' No, He is not slack and neither will I be slack, dear Lord."

It was settled, and Helen did not know that while she slept, a tired mother in the house by the alley was lying awake thinking, thinking—thinking of a girlhood experience and a certain promise.

The dress was cut and ready for stitching by nine o'clock the next morning. Some ripping had to be done more than once and Helen's fingers trembled, but the mother was so kind and patient, so sure it would be just all right, and she didn't know when she could ever get at it herself.

"Helen," whispered Gertrude, just before dinner, "I haven't seen mother so happy in a long time."

The dinner was simple, but good. Helen wondered if she could enjoy taffy any more than she enjoyed that vegetable soup and homemade bread, and chocolate pie. Fourteen eyes cast shy glances at Helen from across the table. The baby boy chuckled in his basket by the stove.

At three o'clock came a long-distance call. The mother answered.

"Who? Yes, Jennie! What? Our Bobbie died? I can't hardly hear—" Yes, John will be home. We'll leave in about an hour and a half."

"What??" asked the children as they gathered around their mother crying and fearful.

"Oh!" sobbed the mother, "Oh, No!" Jeannie's little boy—died—died of pneumonia this noon!" Oh, what will

Jennie do, her only child and he was the sweetest little fellow with golden curls all over his head."

"Bobbie? Bobbie dead?" Cried their mother. The children gathered in, clinging close to their mother.

"Why, I didn't even know he was so sick. I can't believe it! I can't!! Oh, no!!"

"What is dead?" Asked little Johnnie tearfully. It must be something awful to make Mommy cry so hard.

"Oh, Johnnie," She took him in her arms. "It's when you go to sleep and never wake up any more."

"Never?"

"Not on this earth, but little children wake up—in—heaven where—"

"Where their mothers are—huh, Mama?"

"Oh, Johnnie, yes, if they—oh, I must get ready. Daddy will soon be here. Oh, Helen, how can I ever thank you for coming over and sewing for me today? The good Lord knew I would need that dress by tonight. What would I have done without you?"

"I'm glad I came," Helen's voice was soft. I was invited to a taffy pull, but last night I promised God I would keep my promise to Gertrude and come over here today. If I had not kept my promise, I would never have forgiven myself. I can go to lots of taffy-pulls. I will have the dress finished by the time you are ready to leave."

The mother stood fixed as one in a dream, with her eyes on Helens face. Suddenly hot gushing tears blinded her eyes and she sank into a chair and sobbed as if her heart would break.

"When—when I was sixteen, my mother and—I—I—promised I'd become a Christian before her next birthday, and—and I did not keep my promise. Would to God I could go back and keep it. How different some things would have been. Oh, Helen, Gertrude, children, let me tell you all right now, if you make a promise, and it's a good one, keep it—kept it I say."

"It's not to late to keep your promise," Said Helen, putting her arms around the mother's shoulder. You can be a Christian now before your next birthday."

Then a silence. At last the woman made a great sigh as if relieved of some tremendous burden.

"I will," she whispered. "God help me. If a girl can give up a party to make a dress for a struggling mother who broke her promise, year after year, I want to love and serve her God, too. I promise God right now. And, Helen, you stay here with the children till we get back? It will be quite late, but we'll be back tonight. It's twenty miles. Oh, Jennie, and dear little Bobbie! Will you stay here and comfort my babies, Helen, and tell them about heaven and explain to them what it means to die?"

"I will. I'll promise to do all I can."

About the Author

*M*arcia Kauffman Clark is the youngest of Nelson Edward and Christmas Carol Kauffman's four children. She moved with her parents and brother James Milton, to Elkhart, Indiana in August 1956. Marcia sang in a sextet with the same six girls all four years while attending Bethany Christian High School in Goshen, Indiana. She attended Hesston College in Hesston Kansas for two years and graduated with a Secondary Education Degree in Home Economics in 1965 from Goshen College, Goshen, Indiana. The greatest highlight of her high school and college years was singing and especially with the traveling choirs while in college. Marcia moved to Phoenix, Arizona, in 1969. She has enjoyed teaching, singing, sewing, and creative writing. She sang first alto in a ladies quartette for twenty- one years. She had the opportunity of traveling in Europe twice as a ten-year member of the Sonoran Desert Chorale. She and her husband, Stephen, live in Tempe, Arizona, and have eight children, twenty-three grandchildren, and three great-grandsons.

Marcia Kauffman Clark can be reached by mail at:

1026 East Alameda Drive
Tempe, Arizona 85282

Word Possible

W hen I was young, Mother created a game that we played in our home.

We call the game *Word Possible—A Game with over Twelve Thousand Possible Answers*. It will soon be published and available through Digital Legend Press.

Ten reasons this game will be a favorite in your home and family:

1. Develops Creative Thinking skills.
2. Can be played with all ages.
3. Good Healthy competition.
4. Different each time it is played.
5. Develops memory skills for both young and old.
6. A great family game and can be played any where.
7. Can be played with any number of players
8. Can be minutes or hours of fun.
9. Brings happiness to all— a circle of joy.
10. The game is forever playable even if cards are lost.